The

PROMISE
of WATER

To Deb:
my dear lifetime
friend. It meant
a lot to me to have
you here Oct 26, 2017
Love
Judy

The
PROMISE
of WATER

by

Judy LeBlanc

OOLICHAN BOOKS
FERNIE, BRITISH COLUMBIA, CANADA
2017

Library and Archives Canada Cataloguing in Publication

LeBlanc, Judy, author

    The promise of water / Judy LeBlanc.

Short stories.

ISBN 978-0-88982-320-4 (softcover)

    I. Title.

PS8573.E249P76 2017   C813'.54   C2017-905060-5

Cover design by Greg Glover www.gregglover.com

We gratefully acknowledge the financial support of the Canada Council for the Arts, the British Columbia Arts Council through the BC Ministry of Tourism, Culture, and the Arts, and the Government of Canada through the Canada Book Fund, for our publishing activities.

Published by
Oolichan Books
P.O. Box 2278
Fernie, British Columbia
Canada V0B 1M0

www.oolichan.com

Printed in Canada

for Russ
in loving memory

Contents

Your Brother Returns in a Canoe   9

Can't Go Wrong with an Iris   15

The Confusion Technique   32

Exposure   51

On the Heron's Watch   67

Paddling Against the Ferryman   81

Crow   97

Erosion   108

Speaking Underwater   119

The Promise of Water   129

Her Father's Jilted Lover   142

Senanus Island   160

This Karst Landscape   167

The Truth about Gravity   181

Filter Feeders   187

Fenced In   195

Your Brother Returns in a Canoe

Your dead brother walks toward you on the beach.

"It's time you got here; there's been nothing but trouble with Mom," you say.

He stops in front of you, drops his crossed arms to his side, tilts his head and smiles as if he saw you only yesterday. There's colour in his cheeks and not a trace of grey in his hair. He looks better than he did in those last days in the hospital when his skin was a pale membrane stretched over bone.

You want to welcome him back, but what slips out in your excitement is, "Nice dye job." It used to irritate him when you said that. Why did you say that?

He touches his head and grins; tiny lines and a dimple appear at the corners of his mouth. The night he died, after not speaking for hours, he'd opened his eyes, clicked his tongue and said, "I told you I didn't want company." Then he'd stroked his chin like he wished he'd had time to shave.

You glance behind you on the bank as if expecting to see his car parked there, but what you see cradled in the branches of a gnarled and monstrous cedar is a canoe. As far as you know your brother never set foot in a canoe.

Or maybe, instead of the beach, he walks into the Starbucks in that cold city where he lived all those years out east away from you, away from family. When he first died, you thought his absence was some kind of trick and you might find him there.

He comes through the door, his face swathed in a scarf mummy fashion and a toque pulled down his forehead, so there's only his eyes: green and blue like the Pacific. He wears a heavy coat the same as those worn by soldiers in the First World War, and though it's shapeless, shroud-like, you assure yourself there's a living breathing body beneath. You flip your laptop closed on that deadline you know you won't now make. And you aren't so much surprised to see him as relieved that he's dressed against the cold.

Unwinding his scarf, he says, "I still hate these fucking winters."

"I still hate this fucking coffee." It's how you speak to each other. Spoke to each other: words like flint.

"Fine. Go back to your micro-roasters and your west coast breweries." His hand is a fan disturbing the air, then a stop sign. Instead of leaving, with the tip of your finger you reach for the spot under his chin where there should be a pulse. Of course he vanishes when you touch him, just as he did when he was alive.

You prefer the beach scenario. He wears a cotton sweater the soft grey of the morning fog and he sits on the rock beside you. The sun will burn off the fog and fill the sky with light; then you'll invite him to join you back at the house on the patio. You'll make him a gin and tonic—he always liked a gin and tonic on a summer day. He'll stretch his long body out on the lounge chair and you'll remind him of that time when you were kids and you built a raft from logs on the beach; you were going to sail to China. He'll admire the new house, your very own since the divorce. You'll tell him he was right about your ex. You'll have another drink and tell him his nephew is in university now. A lot of years have passed. You won't ask him about where he's been. Though you're curious, it seems an invasion of privacy to interview a man about his afterlife—and maybe you don't want to know.

"What's going on with Mom?" He picks up a rock and turns it over in his hand.

It so happens that you've been thinking about rocks, how they embed their deep geology in telltale striations while changing their appearance and shape over millennium. In that sense, if they were alive, they would never actually die. You might explain this to him, but you are reluctant to speak of death.

He didn't like to talk about death when he was alive. He'd sooner talk about everyday things: the rudeness of the fat woman at the checkout in Loblaws, how she twitched her nose at him like a rabbit and wouldn't honour his expired rain check. You would point out the inarguable fact of an expiration date, but he would obsess about these kinds of affronts for hours, the checker becoming more gargoyle-like with every telling so that the event morphed into a black comedy and in the end he'd have you laughing. Or he'd roll his eyes at your husband or your kids, how you handled some domestic problem and he liked to give advice that you sometimes took even though you considered him clueless about the tedium and heartaches of family life.

Heartaches he knew though he spoke of them rarely, and usually only with the assistance of plenty of burgundy-coloured wine. A year before he died your brother returned from a holiday—he was always going south to Tiquana, to Acapulco, leaving Toronto behind then returning—to find his partner had rented a basement suite in a neighbourhood far from the Beaches where the two of them had lived for eight long years. The partner, a man not nearly as good-looking as your brother, had moved all of your brother's things into this apartment and demanded the keys to the house in the Beaches. This struck you as an act of cruelty, but unlike the incident in the grocery store, your brother saw his former lover's actions as justified and reasonable, and in spite of them, maybe because of them, he continued to be in love with this man.

But now you don't want him to talk about these things—they are in the past—you want to keep him focused on the business of your mother. "What's going on with Mom is old age, mostly," you say.

Of course he looks puzzled. What would he know of aging? You say nothing because you don't want to sound resentful.

His gaze shifts across the beach to the low tide line and you feel uncomfortable because that's the place where your mother and you spread his ashes years before.

"She wants to die," you say.

He whirls his head around and for a second you're afraid it might spin full circle on his neck like that scene in *The Exorcist*, but it stops at his shoulder.

"She told everyone she had cancer. So Auntie went out and rented a Karaoke machine and set it up in Mom's apartment. She propped Mom up in the recliner with pillows and blankets. Then Auntie made us listen to her sing, 'Wind Beneath my Wings,' you know... "

"The divine Miss M." He smiles and sings Bette's song, carrying a tune in a way he never could when he was alive, and you feel some of the old jealousy. He finishes one verse and says, "What did Mom do?"

"She threw a hot water bottle at the machine and told Auntie to leave, just leave."

He laughs. "What a bitch."

"Then I phoned her doctor even though she hates me talking to him. He said she didn't have cancer, but that she should quit smoking."

Your brother wouldn't have bothered phoning the doctor. You see now that it was only because he was the youngest. Still, habit makes you say, "It's not fair that everything falls on my shoulders."

He shrugs. "Not much I can do from here." He's said this before.

"She carts that oxygen tank around in one hand and a cigarette in another. She's going to blow herself up."

He pats the place where he once kept a pack of cigarettes in his breast pocket. Your mom and he shared that: the smoking. You could hear them laughing on the back porch while you did the dishes in the kitchen.

"She's never been the same... " You don't finish what you were going to say. "You could go visit her, couldn't you?" You've said this before.

He grins and looks at you from the corner of his eyes. He opens his mouth and inside it's hollow as a cave. "I do."

"She never tells me."

"You'd tell her it was impossible."

You are both silent for a moment.

"All she does is cry," he says.

"Some things never change."

"And then they do."

You trace a stick in the sand and see that his feet have disappeared. You panic because you haven't yet gone for the gin and tonic. There are things you didn't say before and you want to say now. There're things you want to know. "Is there anything you need?"

He looks puzzled again. "What will you do about Mom?" he asks.

"What can I do?" Surely now, after where he's been he

must know something, have access to answers, some certainty that you don't.

He shrugs. Beyond him far out on the water you catch a glimpse of a canoe rocking in the waves, as if it's waiting for a passenger. Your brother is submerged in a cloud, above which floats his head and shoulders. "It's up to her," he says.

"Should we go for a swim before you leave?" You used to like to swim together.

He shakes his head. He no longer has a tongue or a mouth, only an empty space there. The wind catches what's left of him like it did his ashes.

You stand and scan the blank surface of the sea. "It wasn't anything I said, was it?"

But he's gone and you'll never know for sure.

Can't Go Wrong with an Iris

They could drown like this—she and the baby, half-buried in a basement suite, rain nattering and wind whipping at the window above their heads. Daphne sits in the bed with her back against a chilly wall. The baby's head falls away from her breast and she lifts her closer. The child is fecund with the bad and sweet odors of the body: a swamp of milk and urine. Daphne fumbles out of bed and places her in a bassinette. She can't stop looking. It's like watching fish in a tank, eyes attuned to the minutest quiver.

It's 6 am and she knows she won't sleep now. She's been up most of the night. It was a shock at first, this child's need. Shivering, she eases a hoodie over her head and is grateful for flannel pyjama bottoms. Before pulling the string attached to the bulb in the ceiling she glances in the mirror. The purple stripe in her dark hair has faded to a dull violet, and a tiny gold ring clutches the flesh beneath her nostrils. When she was a little girl, she had wanted to be a gypsy, wear bangles and dance all night. Beneath the hoodie, she grabs belly fat and bounces her breasts with the palm of her other hand. She's a big-titted cow. That's what she is. She shakes her head and yanks the string. The room turns grey. She needs a cigarette.

Water has seeped in under the outside door and the stink of mould rises from the sopping wall-to-wall. The landlord hadn't mentioned the place flooded. Jerk. Can she dry it before Sebastian's mom arrives?

In the room that is both living room and kitchen, she digs through one of the boxes for towels. She layers them on the floor and the water oozes upward into a dark stain. It reminds her of the house she and Eden lived in that winter in Esquimalt, how they had to scoop water from the drain outside the basement door. And the rats, how they scratched and scampered behind the walls at night. It made it scarier that she never actually saw one. "They won't hurt you," Eden said, but Daphne could tell that her mother was just as freaked as she was.

According to Daphne's social worker from the Young Mom's Program, this place is decent and worth the forty dollars above her shelter allowance. It has a bedroom and she can walk to Beacon Hill Park with the baby. She'll find a way to get the forty bucks. As for the flood, the landlord is just going to have to rent her a carpet cleaner and fix the drain outside the door. She weaves through the piles of boxes, some neatly stacked, some open to a jumble of her belongings: flipflops, pilled sweaters, pamplets from the Health Authority on pregnancy and childbirth, a collection of plastic My Little Pony toys, their neon-coloured bodies an affront in the dim light of the apartment.

Dropping onto a chair, she scoops up her cellphone and checks messages. There is one from Brittany. "Hey, Daph, wish you were here. We got a fire going on the beach. Just a minute. What?" Giggling, and a guy's voice in the background. Daphne can't make out what he's saying. "Josh has got some wicked brew." More giggling. "Daph, about tomorrow night, don't hate me. I can't help you unpack. My mom is making me go to my uncle's for dinner. Shit. I know I cancelled last time. I feel so guilty. Love ya."

"Airhead," says Daphne. She can't remember Eden,

her mother, "make her" do anything, though it must
have happened. No messages from Sebastian. Why would
there be? Sebastian is not the kind to drunk-dial. Sebastian
is not the kind to get drunk. Lately, he hasn't been the kind
to phone at all.

Sebastian had texted the day the baby was born: *Brittany
said a girl. Sorry not there. Final exams.* She'd flung the phone
onto the floor beside the hospital bed and had one of those
big snot-nosed cries into her pillows. With the way she carried
on it's a good thing no one was there. Snorting and tearing
at her hair like a mad woman. They would have thought she
was so immature. She didn't want anyone talking adoption
again. By the time the nurse brought the baby, Daphne was
able to look up from the magazine on her lap, and crack a
big smile.

Three days later, after she was discharged from the hospital,
when she hadn't heard from him, she texted Sebastian back:
Since UR so smart, help me name baby? His text followed within
minutes: *Can do. Mom wants to meet you. Wednesday, 9:00?*

Wow. She dialed his number. No answer. She left a message.
"I can't believe it. She wants to meet her granddaughter. That's
so cool. I thought she hated me. Are you coming with her? I
won't put any pressure on you. I'm over it. You know that.
But you should see your daughter. She's so sweet."

She's lost track of how many times she's texted or left
messages since then. She hated it, and she knew he did too,
when girls power-dialed their boyfriends. He wasn't her
boyfriend. He'd only been her boyfriend for three months
and it was over last September. It was now June. It was over
before she knew she was pregnant. Not that she hadn't told
him the minute she knew. She's nobody's fool. She wouldn't
get an abortion, and he wanted her to. He said because she

refused, he wasn't responsible. He was so stupid that way. The social worker told her she had to fill out forms and he'd be forced to pay support for the baby. She'd have to do this if she wanted welfare.

"Sebastian is seventeen years old. He's never even worked at McDonalds," she'd said to the social worker.

"He's seventeen and jobless *now*. Do you think that's going to last?"

The least he could do is help her name the baby. He said he would. He was good at naming things. Last night she texted: *Augusta venerable?* She'd copied it from the baby name book. Sebastian would know what venerable meant and think that she didn't. By 4:00 she'd changed her mind about *Augusta*. She didn't want a child that expected to be treated like a queen. *Bella intelligent?*, she typed. Eden always tells Daphne that she's too smart for her own good. Daphne wants a smart daughter.

The pipes above her head gurgle and spew with the contents of a flushing toilet. Upstairs, it's dry. They're all university students up there, three or four of them, older than she is, living on top of her. She thinks there are two girls and one guy, but there's so many people coming and going that she's not sure. She's only been here two weeks. Once at the garbage can, she came face-to-face with a skinny blonde girl. Daphne held the lid so the girl could drop her bag into the can. The girl smiled, sort of, didn't thank her.

The wind has died and the rain subsided into a soft background hiss. The metallic click of her lighter startles the silence and she thinks that she might have woken the baby, though no sound comes from the bedroom. She lights the cigarette, checks dialed and received calls to see if the landlord's number is there. Nothing. Maybe she's erased it.

Her social worker would have it because she helped her find the place. She likes her social worker even though her hair is frizzy and lined with grey, so big it seems to interfere with their conversations. Daphne wants to take a flat iron to it. The worker asks questions like a CCSIS interrogator, but you could rob a bank and she'd tell you she knew you meant well. Is she coming today or tomorrow? Daphne digs the calendar out from under a pile of kitchen utensils. This afternoon—2:00. For the ten days since the baby was born, Daphne has drawn a happy face on the calendar. She draws another one on today's date and counts the days, shocked at how much she wants this child.

She drags on her cigarette and puts her feet on a box, knocking over a bag full of food stained wrappers from McDonalds. Leona is Sebastian's mom's name. It means *lioness,* or so it says in the baby book. "Like you," Sebastian once said, and she took it as a compliment.

Who comes for a visit at 9 am? You go to appointments at 9 am. Did Leona take the morning off just to meet Daphne and her new granddaughter? It's weird that now, finally, she wants to meet her. In the summer when she and Sebastian were dating, Leona and Sebastian's dad were in Europe. Sebastian had volunteered at a science program and stayed at his Aunt's house. When his parents got back, he made excuses for not introducing them to her. Daphne doesn't know when he finally told Leona about the baby. Maybe only after the baby was born. His family is different from hers, and she doesn't always understand the way things are supposed to be done in families. Leona is not like Eden. She takes her responsibilities seriously. Even if her son is a shithead.

Daphne butts her cigarette into an empty cup. She'll find the teapot before Leona comes. She'll clear the counter and tidy up the boxes. She'll get some stuff unpacked before the baby wakes up, maybe even bathe her, show Leona she's no loser. She'll tell her how the worker is going to get her into college and she's going to have a good job like Leona's one day when the baby is older. Leona will help her the way she helps Sebastian. She'll take care of the baby sometimes. Sebastian's a shithead, but he's decent because he comes from a decent family. He just needs to mature. Leona can see that. She probably tells him to call Daphne back.

Daphne went to their house once. A couple of months ago, she showed up at the school and followed Sebastian home. He wouldn't walk with her for the first few blocks. Though he didn't admit it, she knew he was embarrassed about her big stomach. Later, he seemed to forget about it.

His parents had been at work and he lit a fire in the wood stove in the TV room. They lay on the leather couch. Daphne imagined the big bowl of popcorn on the coffee table, Leona's hand resting on her son's shoulder, and during the commercials—his dad making jokes.

They were tangled in a nest of blankets and clothes, her round belly gleaming in the dim light. He buried his face in her hair, and his voice was muffled. "If only my mom could meet you."

"Then what?"

He slid his hand over the dome of her belly. She imagined the baby pressing against it, drawn to his palm's warmth. Asking him out had been a dare; he wore t-shirts with collars and carried a briefcase, was a straight A student and won the science award every year. A geek and yet he was the fastest runner in the school, his skin smooth and olive-toned, his eyes a deep, deep brown. Her friends teased her about taking away his virginity. She didn't tell them it had been a mutual exchange.

She took a handful of the curls that sat on his head like a crown.

"Ouch," he said.

"Sissy."

He pushed himself up and placed his chin in his hand, all the time tracing her belly with his finger. His voice droned as though he were in a trance. "Hey little fish girl, I know you're in there, swimming in your amniotic pond. Pigging out on proteins, carbohydrates. Can you hear me greedy little fish girl?" He glanced at Daphne and then pressed his ear to her belly. "She's got everything she needs."

"She's safe."

"Safe." He nodded and splayed his hand across her belly just as it bulged on Daphne's right side below her ribs. "There she is. There she is, give me a kiss, Baby." His lips smacked her belly.

Laughing, she pushed him away. "You'll hurt us."

He got up and stoked the fire, put a blanket over them. She was warm. She left before his parents got home.

He liked to educate her. Before she was pregnant, he took her for a walk in Mt. Doug Park. He crouched at the edge of the tangled mass of vegetation along the trail and identified plants by name: *kinnikinnick, Oregon grape, sword fern.* Then he tested her to see if she could remember. When she couldn't he came up behind her, slipped his hand under her shirt, gripped just below her belly and pulled her against him.

"Just not as smart as you, I guess," she said. "I'm not a geek."

"But you are named after an invasive species." His voice was a near whisper.

"What?"

He grinned then kissed her neck.

"I don't know what you mean," she said.

He stepped back and gestured to the side of the trail.

"Spurge Daphne." He pointed at a squat shiny-leaved shrub. She bent to pluck a leaf and he said, "Don't. It's poisonous."

"It doesn't look poisonous. There's lots of it."

"It may look innocent but it's threatening an entire ecosystem; that's how dangerous it is."

"Spurge Daphne. My mother named me after an invasive, poisonous species."

He laughed.

A hollowness flooded her belly and pressed upward tightening her throat. She bit her lip. She wouldn't cry in front of him. He stepped away from her.

"I didn't mean anything," he said. "It was a joke." He held up his hands. "Your mom didn't know."

"Eden knew," she said.

The rest of that day he called her his rare fawn lily, bought her ice cream and rode home with her on the bus. He wanted to be a biologist, maybe save the world someday. There was something *that* good about him and she had wanted that goodness to wash over her and leave its trace.

Daphne dries the dishes and stacks them in the tiny cupboard. It's 8:00 am, a faint light coming through the windows. She'll have to buy curtains. She puts the teapot on the counter beside a box of teabags. She still has to find the kettle. The baby will wake soon. Her breasts are tingling. Time for a quick shower but first, a smoke. She's put the two chairs on either side of a large box that'll serve as a table for now. She lights a cigarette and opens the baby name book. Then she grabs the cellphone. *Lily*, she types, and *send*. She jumps when the phone rings. "Hello."

"Hey, Baby, how are you?" It's her mother's high-pitched whine.

"Eden."

"I swear the raindrops are bigger here, Hon. It hasn't stopped for three days."

"Yeah."

"How's the baby?"

"She's fine."

"Have you got a name for her yet?"

"No."

"Daph! Annie and I will put our heads together."

"It's okay."

"You mad at me?"

"Always," says Daphne.

"Give me a break. Things are going to be good, here. Tofino has changed so much from when you were a baby."

"I don't remember it."

"Well, I know you don't. Look, I'm learning so much from Annie about reflexology."

"Yeah."

"Anyway, I want you and the baby to come visit. I want to meet my granddaughter. It's kind of cramped on the boat but maybe I'll have my own place soon."

"I don't have any money, Mom, and the baby's too young."

"It's not like she's going to break, Daph. You didn't."

"You sending me the money for the bus?"

"You know I don't have any. Annie is going to set me up..."

"I gotta go. The baby's awake."

"Alright, Sweetie, I just wanted you to know I'm thinking about you."

The last time Daphne saw Eden was a month ago at the House of Eggplant, her mom's favorite restaurant in Victoria. It's in the basement of an old warehouse down along the water. Eden likes it because they only serve locally grown organic vegan food. Because of her sensitivities, there is a lot of food that Eden's system can't tolerate. Daphne tires of hearing about it. At times Eden doesn't seem quite corporeal to Daphne, as if her bones are made of chiffon. She wraps herself in pashima scarves and wears soft slip-on shoes. Her long hair, once blonde, now darkened with streaks of grey, is usually twisted in braids around her head. Her eyes are pale blue. Daphne feels a need to wear her lace-up leather boots whenever she sees her mother.

They met at noon, Daphne coming from morning classes at the Young Mom's Program, and Eden, well, who knows what Eden did all day? It embarrasses Daphne that her mother has been on welfare most of Daphne's life. At noon, people were crowded into the tiny restaurant.

"How are things at the home?" asked Eden.

"You make it sound like I'm retarded. It's not a home."

"You know what I mean. Are you getting the services you need?"

"The services?"

Eden sipped her apple and ginger drink. She'd asked them to add bee pollen and leave out the beets. "Don't be hostile, Daph. You know you're better off there. You can't be sleeping on the couch when you're pregnant, and they feed you better than I can."

Daphne's back ached and the strong scent of basil and fresh roasted coffee turned her stomach. At the table behind them, a man with a braid in his hair, not much older than Daphne, was delivering a monologue on the evils of the pharmaceutical industry while his girlfriend tried to tell him that she wanted to break up.

"There's something too earnest about this place," said Daphne.

"What does that have to do with anything?"

Her mother was a stupid woman. Daphne chewed on her veggie burger and told herself to be kind.

Eden sighed. "I have an opportunity."

"Really."

"You remember Annie."

"No."

"She loved you when you were a little girl."

"I don't remember being a little girl."

"Well your dad and I... we all lived together in Tofino."

Other than odd reminiscences over the halcyon days before Daphne's second birthday, *Dad* was not part of the family lexicon.

"Yes, so you've said—on the beach in little driftwood shelters—like squatters." She shouldn't have said that.

"Not like squatters."

"Well, kind of."

"Squatters take over other people's land. The colonists were squatters." Eden gripped the edge of the table with both hands.

"Well, didn't you descend from a colonist?"

"It doesn't make me one."

"How's that?"

The man with the braid was telling his girlfriend she should go to a Chinese medicine doctor. His girlfriend was trying to interrupt him and her voice was cracking.

"This is a dumb conversation," said Daphne, and sipped the mint tea Eden had recommended for nausea. She touched her belly. "This works, this tea, I think."

Eden sighed again. "I'm moving back to Tofino."

Daphne put down her burger and stared at her mother. Eden's shoulders had rolled forward, her top teeth bit her bottom lip, and she looked down.

"When?"

"Tomorrow. It's the beginning of the month. I don't want to have to pay rent here. It's so expensive to live here, Daph. And Stephen, Annie's partner, has left and I can stay on the boat with her. She just finished a reflexology course and she'll teach me. I would have told you sooner. Eventually, you're going to have to get your own place, anyway. And I wasn't sure."

Eden wasn't sure about anything.

Eden glanced up. "She's my oldest friend. She needs me."

"Eden, I'm sixteen years old and I'm going to have a baby—Mom."

Eden dug through her purse. Her breathing was shallow. She didn't look at her daughter. "I have something for you."

Daphne had to lean forward to hear her. Eden handed her a tiny necklace.

A pendant containing a pink flower pressed between a bubble of glass, hung from a tiny silver chain.

"She'll have to be older, you know, before she can wear it, of course. Do you remember it, Daph?"

Daphne shook her head.

"I made it for you when you were born. A friend had a rare Daphne plant in Tofino. I loved the flowers. You wore it when you were a little girl. I found it when I was packing. I know it's not enough. I'd give you more if I could."

Daphne looked everywhere but at her mother. What she hated most about the House of Eggplant was that it was below ground, and out the windows, all you could see were the legs of passers by.

Daphne pulls on jeans and a clean sweater, gathers her wet hair into a pony tail. Her breasts are hard and starting to leak. She checks the baby again. Still asleep. Should she wake her so she'll be clean and powdered when Leona arrives? But you aren't supposed to wake babies. She could have everything ready for the baby, be organized. She leans over the tub and runs water into the baby's basin, checks the temperature the way they'd taught her at the hospital. But this is dumb. The water will get cold before the baby wakes up. It's 8:45.

She'd forgotten about the towels in front of the door. She hurries to the front door and scoops them into her arms: a sopping, smelly mess that drips onto her jeans. "Fuck." When she dumps them into the bathtub muddy water splashes into the baby's plastic basin. She rinses it quickly and leans it against the tub. With a pot in hand, she opens the front door. There are three steps down from the backyard into the basement suite and the bottom step is brimming with muddy water. She reaches into the drain and pulls out a mass of leaves. The water gurgles, swirls, then steadies itself. Still at least a couple of inches deep. She scoops with the pot and at that moment the baby starts to cry and Leona comes around the side of the house.

She's a big woman. A head full of dark hair held back with a metal hair band gives the impression of a mane. A bouquet of flowers and two bulging shopping bags fill her arms. Her smile is a quick upward shift of the lips. Daphne stands. Mud slides down her arms.

"You must be Daphne." She holds out her hand. Daphne glances at her own muddy hand, wipes it quickly on her jeans and takes Leona's; it's big and soft like a paw, doesn't grasp so much as stroke.

"I hear the little one. You get her. I'll come on in if that's okay."

When Daphne comes into the kitchen with the baby, Leona is sitting on one of the chairs, wiping her nylon feet with Kleenex. "You've had a flood, I see. You'll need to call the landlord. He'll have to fix that. I don't like it when landlords take advantage... "

Her eyes stop on the bundle Daphne holds against her naked

breast. The muscles around Leona's mouth soften. She looks away and returns to wiping her feet. It seems to Daphne it shouldn't take that long to dry her feet.

"Sorry, I should have told you to leave your shoes on," says Daphne. "I know to talk to the landlord. He won't get my rent cheque unless he fixes it."

Leona jerks her head up, studies Daphne's face. "Well, yes, it's important to protect yourself."

"I know how to do that," Daphne says.

The baby suckles and the two women fix their eyes on one another. Daphne will not look away.

"You're a strong girl," says Leona.

"I've had to be." She is happy that Leona sees this about her.

Leona glances out the window. Her jaw tightens. "I have to make all Sebastian's decisions for him." Her voice drops into a mumble, then she turns to Daphne with a large lioness smile. "Well, baby's healthy?"

"Almost nine pounds already. She's got an appetite."

"Children do." Leona's eyes flit to the tiny head at Daphne's breast. "You know I'd love to hold her, but I've had this cold." She spreads five fingers and pushes at the air, a gesture Daphne recognizes from Sebastian. She has his coloring and the shape of his nose, but not his eyes. Hers are narrower, paler.

"There's tea," says Daphne. "I can make it. I'm getting good at doing things with one hand."

"That's okay, Hon. Actually, I don't have a lot of time but I did want to bring you some things."

A bouquet of irises lie on the counter, newspaper wrapped around their stems, and above purple petals. "The flowers are pretty, thank you."

"Oh, that's nothing. Let me put them in water for you. Do you have a vase?" She jumps to her feet.

"No, a glass, there in the cupboard." Daphne points.

"They're from my garden. Iris have such delicate petals, yet they are a tough flower. You can't go wrong with an iris." She fills a glass with water, chops the ends of the stems, and arranges the flowers inside. At that moment, sunlight breaks between the clouds and shoots through the window, washing the petals in a purple glow. Both women notice.

"Oh, Daphne, they're so pretty," says Leona. She claps her hands.

Daphne smiles. The baby is warm against her tummy, her lips soft and motionless on her nipple, satisfied. "I don't know what to name her," says Daphne.

"You'll think of something." Leona, all bustle and business, reaches for one of the bags beside the chair. "You'll need clothes. They grow out of things so fast. I'd forgotten how much fun it is to shop for baby clothes."

From the bags, she pulls piles of colourful terrycloth sleepers, lace and silk dresses, little cotton jackets, all fresh and clean with the tags still dangling from them. She holds them up one by one for Daphne to admire. She emphasizes their quality and durability, colour schemes and washing instructions.

Daphne mumbles her appreciation and when the baby wakes, shifts her to her other breast.

Leona folds each piece of clothing and places them back in the bags. She glances at her watch.

"How's Sebastian?" says Daphne. "I thought he might come to see the baby." She hadn't thought that for a minute.

"Exams, you know. Anyway, I'm not sure it's a good idea." Leona shakes her head. "He's not as mature as you. I can see that now." Her eyes sweep the room: the boxes, the flood, then settle on the baby and on Daphne.

"And he's doing so well right now. You know he's applied to McGill. He'll have no trouble getting in. Sebastian has always been an honour student. He's gifted, you know."

"Is McGill in Montreal?"

"Yes, Hon. Oh, I'll miss him but a mother can't just think of her own needs. She has to think of what's good for her child." She glances again at the baby. Her face reddens and she bites her lip.

"Would you like to hold her?"

"No." She waves her hand. "I don't want to make her sick." She hesitates then stands up. "I have something else for you." She digs around her purse and pulls out her wallet.

The baby yanks her head away from Daphne's breast and wails.

"Shhhh." Daphne burps her the way she's been shown and the baby messes her diaper excreting a foul smell into the space between the two women. Leona places a cheque on the box that is a stand-in for a kitchen table. Daphne shuffles the baby back to her breast but the baby is restless and irritable.

"Daphne," says Leona, leaning towards her now and speaking above the baby's wail. "He has a future."

For a second she thinks Leona is talking about the baby, and she wants to correct her; to say, "It's a she."

Daphne doesn't get up when Leona gathers her bag and wishes her well. She says nothing when Leona stops at the door and faces the outside. Hesitates.

Daphne's eyes are on the cheque. Her mouth is dry and she feels her heart push inside her chest, blood pumping; she has been tuned to her body for nine months. The baby squirms and her limbs stiffen, hands tighten to fists and the little face flushes red. She wails, gasps and wails again. Daphne carries her to the door. Leona has gone around the house. The baby thrashes her tiny limbs in circles and Daphne loosens her grip. Stupid child could fall to the ground, fold into the drain, dissolve into water beneath the house and become the flood that oozes into this basement winter after winter.

"Fuck this," says Daphne. She takes the screaming baby

back to the bedroom and lays her in the bassinette. She grabs her leather boots from the front door, and pushes her feet inside. Without lacing them, she hurries through the door to the front yard. Leona, in her Saab, is pulling away from the curb. Daphne struts across the sidewalk, laces slapping the pavement, toward the car. Leona looks up and waves, puts her foot on the gas. Inside the house the baby screams. Smoke puffs from the Saab's exhaust. Daphne bites her fist. She's shaking. The Saab, with Leona in it, disappears around the next block. Daphne has left an imprint of teeth in her flesh. She closes her eyes and breathes the way they taught her in pre-natal class. When the trembling stops, she opens her eyes. She hears her daughter.

The Confusion Technique

The top of Brindle's head grazes the doorframe as he walks into the kitchen. The knife in its leather sheaf wobbles against his black lace-up boots. Amy draws her eyes away from it before she says good morning and tries not to think about Brindle's file—how it states, in bureaucratic-speak, that when he was four years old he watched his father kill his mother.

Not that he says good morning back. He goes to the cereal cupboard and pulls out a box of Cheerios, a box of Shreddies and a box of Corn Puffs, holds them in his arms as if holding a baby and then drops them on the table across from her. No words. No eye contact. Other than what she's read and what the social worker has told her, she's learned this much about him in the four weeks since she became a group home parent. Brindle likes his cereal mixed.

She's curled on the kitchen chair with her long legs pulled to her chest. She should eat, skinny as she is, but she's not hungry. She's tired this morning after last night, and she doesn't want to make the effort to talk to Brindle because she'll end up feeling like she always does: that she's peppering him with questions that do nothing to make inroads. Making inroads is what they taught her to do in the Child and Youth Care program from which she graduated with honors five years before.

The degree, the on-call relief work she did in other group homes and her former job as a Youth street worker got her this position as houseparent. As for Thesp, her boyfriend and fellow houseparent, sometimes when he heads out in the morning on his way to his job at Lug-A-Rug where he wraps himself in a carpet and waves at traffic on Blanshard Street, she wonders why he was hired. She supposes it was because the Ministry for Children and Families wants couples and because he doesn't have a criminal record. It's not exactly a job that's in high demand.

Last summer Thesp wore a top hat and tails, affected an English accent, and sold tickets to tourists for the Tally Ho carriage ride. He calls himself an actor in training. He doesn't seem to realize the kids in the group home laugh at him, not with him. She ignores them when they call him, "Shag Boy," and comforts herself with the thought that she and Thesp are going to save their money from the group home job so that he can study theatre.

Thesp is short for Thespian—not his real name. "I'm reinventing myself," he'd said at sixteen when Amy first met him. He was going to Oak Bay High at the time, and she didn't really know what he meant, but listening to him, she thought he sounded philosophical. It wasn't how people talked at her school. She went to Colquitz, or Call-it-quits as it was commonly known. Amy's brother quit in grade ten and went up north to Fort Smith where he got a job at a truck stop restaurant bussing tables. Now he manages a hotel there. He emails Amy and says he could get her on serving tables or cleaning rooms. Sometimes she thinks of dumping Thesp and heading up to join her brother. She'd like to lie on the snow and watch the aurora borealis sweep the sky, light up that darkest season. She's seen it on YouTube.

Brindle's bangs shift like a curtain at an open window, sometimes giving you a glimpse of his eyes. He lowers his head to his cereal and hunches his shoulders, chewing slowly with his mouth closed. He's like a turtle disappearing into its shell, but after he's finished, he'll ask if he can be excused and will takes his bowl to the counter. The other two group home kids never do that, but they know better than to mock him for it.

He's late for his employment program again and Amy feels this pressure to say something. The first time she knew he was late, she pretended to forget what time his program started. He'd simply answered, "It starts at 9:00." It was 10:30. "Oh," she'd said. Then one time she asked him, "Aren't you late?" She hated how singsong her voice sounded. He'd finished chewing and without looking up said, "yes." He'll be eighteen in a few months and have to move out of the group home, so what's there to say.

She cradles her cup of coffee in the same way Shelagh held the beaker last night. Amy hadn't thought to ask her where she got it, though now thinks Shelagh must have stolen it from the science lab at Mt. Doug High.

Shelagh shares an attic bedroom with Tanis who has a tally mark scraped on her body for every foster home she's been in since she was six years old. Little clusters of four horizontal lines bisected with slash marks appear like stitches when she rolls up a sleeve or a pant leg. There's three on the back of her neck that Amy quickly counts when Tanis flips up her hair: five, ten, fifteen. Scar tissue.

The night before, Shelagh came in drunk three hours after curfew, and Amy followed her up the narrow stairwell to the girls' bedroom. Shelagh's tiny with tight curls like an elf, fit and agile, a basketball star at her old school. She had wobbled, veered against the wall and doubled over giggling. Amy caught her before she stumbled, shushed and warned her not to wake Tanis. The light flooded through the opening at the top where the stairs stopped in the middle of their bedroom.

The older girl lay stretched out on her bed fully dressed in jeans and a sweatshirt with her hands folded on her stomach. Motionless except for when she turned her head to look first at Shelagh, then at Amy, eyes slits on her doughy face.

Shortly after Amy and Thesp took the job, Amy had asked Tanis what kept her awake night after night. Tanis had gripped her bottom lip in her top teeth, wrapped a beefy arm around Amy's neck, released her, then left the room laughing.

Last night Tanis would have probably belted Shelagh if Amy hadn't been there though, truthfully, Amy doesn't know if Tanis would alter her behaviour for anyone.

"What the fuck?" Tanis had shouted, sitting up and bending her knees.

Shelagh lurched toward the dresser and grabbed the empty beaker. She held it firmly between two hands, a tribute to her basketball skills. Then she dropped her head forward and puked with absolute precision. She filled the beaker to the rim, and the stink of vomit exploded in the room. Her hands remained rock solid steady around the beaker, her face scrunched in pure concentration. She glanced at Tanis and licked the vomit that traced her lips.

"For fuck sake, get it out of here."

Shelagh whipped her head upward and, with eyes closed, raised one leg so that her knee almost touched the bottom of the beaker; Amy half expected her to whinny. She moved like an athlete: each muscle in tune with the others, all physique, all basketball star. Clutching the beaker the whole time, she descended the stairs. Amy followed while Tanis stood cross-armed at the top. On the main floor, Shelagh strode down the hall straight-backed without stirring the beaker's contents, and into the bathroom. She hovered above the toilet then with a whoop of triumph tipped the full beaker into the bowl. In a vaporous cloud of vodka and vomit, she wrapped her arms around Amy. Amy dropped her chin on the girl's head, and caught a whiff of minty shampoo, Shelagh's favourite.

Amy has a weird sensation that her thoughts are drifting outside of her, invisible in the rising steam from the coffee cup she holds close to her face. This sometimes signals the onset of a migraine.

"You should kick Shelagh's ass." Across the table Brindle stares at her, his hair tucked behind his ears and his eyes wide.

This may be the closest thing to an opinion Brindle has expressed to her, maybe the most words he's strung together in the few short weeks she's known him. "Yeah," she says, trying to keep the excitement out of her voice and making it sound like a question. Just enough to encourage him to talk.

"Can I be excused." He mumbles and stands. Without waiting for an answer, he picks up his bowl.

She needs to stop him from leaving just yet, to capitalize on this connectable moment—to make inroads. "What would you do?" She emphasizes the *you*—taking him by surprise—a therapeutic intervention called the "Confusion Technique." She sips her coffee with satisfaction.

Brindle places the bowl back on the table, scratches his chin as if he is considering a difficult physics equation. "I'd kick her ass," he says, nodding his head.

"You mean like actually kick her ass?"

"That's what I said."

"Do you think it would work?"

"Not for me, like if you did it to me, but for her, yes." He takes his bowl and walks to the sink, rinses it out and puts it in the rack.

It occurs to her that she might engage his authority in

the house and get him on side. Another therapeutic technique. "Maybe you should do it," says Amy.

He looks at her with raised eyebrows.

"I mean not literally, not actually, but you know, a kind of big brother thing."

"I'm not her brother." He steps closer. "You do it. Literally," he says, and veers toward the kitchen door.

Amy glances at the clock. He'll be two hours late for his program. She probably should have called him on it. And what was she thinking asking him to do her job? What would the house social worker say? Each day she feels less adequate.

Black lines zigzag across the social worker's face, pulsing patterns around her nose and now her forehead. Amy looks away and lifts her teacup.

Thesp is absent from this Monday meeting, though it has been scheduled intentionally on his day off.

"He's maybe been held up," says Amy. "He had errands to run this morning."

She knows the aura will peak and then pass in minutes so says nothing to the social worker. The migraines are something all her own shared only with Thesp who likes her to describe what she sees. She considers her migraine pain to be the only intimacy remaining between them.

The social worker asks about Shelagh, whose parents have been going to a counsellor and would like to integrate her back into their home as soon as possible, but whether the father will remain in the home is dependent on the results of the police investigation.

"She's a temporary ward and the less time she's in care, the better, but we don't want to send her home too soon."

Today Amy winces at the irony and weight of the phrase,

"in care." She tells the social worker about the girl's recent drunkenness, though leaves out the part about her vomiting in the beaker. The social worker thinks Amy should have grounded Shelagh. This hadn't occurred to Amy who had felt that it was enough that Shelagh cleaned up after herself and made it to school the next day, but of course the social worker is right; really, Shelagh should have felt the full consequences of her behaviour.

The aura lifts from the social worker's face as she begins talking about positive reinforcement for good behaviour. She's suggesting a chart on the fridge, monetary rewards. Amy always feels a little sadness at the disappearance of the zigzag lines, the world before her reconstituted: crumbs on the table from breakfast, the social worker's tightly-set jaw. In the aftermath of the aura, there is a dull pain behind Amy's eyes and nausea in her gut. She's thinking, not about Shelagh and how she can positively reinforce good behaviour, but about what excuse Thesp will have this time. She sees less and less of him every day.

Amy is putting the final touches on a chart for each of her three wards. Today she thinks of them as wards. She has included the following categories: Chores, Punctuality and, after some thought, she decides to include Attitude. She breaks this last one down into sub-categories: Manners, Language, and Respect. She is calling a house meeting during which she'll define these categories and explain that allowance will now be determined by points earned on the chart. She'll warn them that two new youth will move in Monday morning, and that it's important to instill a system before these kids arrive. She'll tell her current wards that she's counting on them to help the newcomers feel at home. This will be the new approach. She is, after all, a professional.

A basketball whizzes through the kitchen door, bounces and hits her on the forehead. Giggling fills the hallway and the front door slams.

"Shit. Are you alright?" Tanis stands at the doorway.

The ball rolls across the floor toward the stove. "You got me," says Amy and feels for a bump.

"Sorry." Tanis picks up the ball and bounces it toward the stove, her awkward footing approximating a dribble.

Shelagh does a slow exaggerated jog into the kitchen and drops her arms around Amy's neck. "Poor Amy, are you okay?"

"Why are you in such a good mood?" Amy sniffs for alcohol and instead gets a nostril full of Chanel No 5.

"I'm teaching Tanis how to play basketball. She can dribble. Look at her."

Tanis stands at the fridge with her head tipped back pouring a carton of milk into her mouth. Instead of swallowing, she allows the milk to dribble down her chin and onto the front of her shirt. She swallows the remainder and drops into a chair next to Amy. "Shelagh's good at basketball and she's such a shrimp," she says.

Shelagh drops her head to one side and narrows her eyes in mock threat. "Least I'm not fat like you." Then she leaps toward the kitchen door. Tanis lunges for her across the table, knocks the chair over and chases her down the hall. Amy gathers up the charts she's been working on and shoves them on top of the fridge. She follows the girls and stands at the door of the living room. Shelagh and Tanis lie sprawled on either end of the sofa.

"You guys," Amy says.

"Girls," says Shelagh.

"Girls, then."

On the TV screen two skinny models wash their hair.

"I like you both."

Tanis looks up. "Huh... "

"Just thought I'd let you know."

"You're weird." Tanis turns back to the TV.

Shelagh rolls off the couch and lands on her back on the floor. "I like you, too, Amy," she says and blows her a kiss.

That night Amy waits up for Brindle. Thesp is in bed. The girls have gone to their room early. She's in the living room reading at midnight when Brindle comes through the front door. He's snuck up on her more than once, though she likes to think it's not intentional. When he appears in the hallway she calls to him. "Will you sit down a minute?"

In the living room, he folds himself into the armchair. She has no idea where he goes at night.

"How was your night?"

"Same as always."

"I was thinking of having a meeting, like a house meeting, with you and the girls, lay out some expectations."

"Some what?"

"Well, you know, to improve some things around here."

"Like what?"

"Chores and that."

"I'll do chores if they do chores." He gestures with his thumb upstairs in the direction of the girl's bedroom.

"Well, we could set that up. You know."

"No, I don't."

"Tie it into allowances."

Dark hair falls in skinny strands across his eyes. "If you're going to do that, there should be punishment," he says.

"What kind of punishment?"

"Like no supper or something. Ground them when they don't do their chores."

"No need for punishment. They just wouldn't get as much allowance. Kind of like a pay cheque."

"Don't you get a pay cheque whether you work or not?"

He's right and Thesp is a good example of the injustice of that. He hasn't laid eyes on the kids for at least three days. "I guess that's true, but what I mean is we'd set it up like a reward system, an exchange system—work for money, which is kind of like a job."

Brindle seems to consider this, furrows his brow and casts a look around the room. "You're too soft," he says. "They should be punished for talking to you like they do."

"Thanks for your concern, Brindle, but I'm alright." Meaning, I know what I'm doing; though, Amy doesn't know what she's doing. Ever, it seems. She's nice, that's all, but you can't make inroads on niceness. "If I get tough," she says, "then I'll have to get tough with you."

"I do nothing wrong."

"You miss your training program."

"My business." He stands. "I'm out of here in six months. So long Ministry. It's been a slice."

"There's one thing I'd like to ask you."

Brindle's stillness like his silence fills a room.

"Please don't wear your knife when you're here. I'm trying to make this feel like a home. People don't carry knives in their home."

"That so?"

"I mean, they shouldn't."

Thesp disappears for three days and Amy gets an email.

Hey Amy,
I'm in Vancouver staying with a friend, not anyone you
know. I can't do what you do, just be there with those
fucked-up kids. Don't get me wrong. I know it's not their

fault. You know what to do and I don't. Not a lot new about that. It would always be like that, wouldn't it – you doing what has to be done and me just following along.

I've been talking to my father again. He'll set me up if I finish my degree: tuition and an apartment. He says I've got to live up to my potential. I know you don't believe it, but I could be anything I want.

It's been a gas. We had some nice times, you and I, and likely, we'll miss each other now and then.

Take care and all the best.

Darren

Amy is at the desk in the tiny office behind the house-parent's bedroom. She pulls her knees up to her chest and wraps her arms around her calves. Darren was Thesp's name before he was Thesp, and while she was living her real life, he was having a "gas." Getting out of her parent's house, going to university, the part-time jobs, loving him the best she could. She's worked hard. She thinks about these things: what makes people hurt, how to stop the hurt and change bad situations. Aren't these, the most difficult of questions, the most important? She writes him an email; *This is not a gas, you clown.*

Two days before the new intakes arrive, the social worker has their files open on the kitchen table. Amy is having difficulty concentrating on what the social worker is saying, though the words are becoming familiar enough that she no longer has to give it her full attention: *placement breakdown, family conflict, sexual abuse, suicidal ideation, self-medication.*

"It's important Thesp is here when I bring them over Monday." The social worker raises one eyebrow.

Amy's been telling her that Thesp has gone to Vancouver to be with his grandfather who's dying. Thesp's grandfather has been dying for several years, but it's the closest thing to the truth Amy can come up with to explain her partner's continued absence at these meetings.

"Why does it matter if he's here? You know I manage group home business," Amy says.

The social worker sighs. "Amy, we hired you as a couple because the kids benefit from having a mother and a father figure in the home."

That's what they were: she and Thesp? "What if you're wrong?"

"Sorry?"

"I mean about the benefits of a mother/father figure, all that stuff." She waves her hand, stops herself from smacking the table. "Isn't it enough that there's one person who cares, who gives a damn about what happens to these kids?" Her voice wavers and she swallows.

"Amy, don't get mushy. We hired you because you're experienced and you're skilled. You're making inroads with these kids."

"Then why do I need Thesp?" Amy's voice is too loud, too hard.

The social worker sighs and leans forward. "You can't do this on your own without losing perspective—burning out." She claps her hands together and holds them up—a prayer gesture. "Listen, Amy. It's the model the Ministry uses, for better or for worse. What's going on here? You and Thesp okay? I haven't seen him in three weeks."

"Because he doesn't live here anymore."

"Shit," says the social worker and slumps in her chair. "Is he coming back?"

Amy's throat is too tight to get words out. She shakes her head.

"You okay?" The social worker's voice is softer than usual.

Amy nods and swipes away a couple of tears.

"Do the kids know?"

Amy shakes her head.

"Does anyone know?"

"My brother."

"You know what this means?" Her ministry voice is back.

"What? Can't you get someone in to help me? A *father figure.*"

"Is this what you want?"

"Is it about me?"

"Absolutely." The social worker slips her papers into her briefcase and lifts her coat from the chair. "Tell you what. I'll postpone the intakes, and you think about whether this is really what you want right now. If you're sure, I'll give some thought to finding a replacement for Thesp."

The migraines return, first the auras then the blade above her eyes. She dreams of two children at a bus stop, one fat with pimples and the other with an earring in her eyebrow. They stand on a winter-hard ground in their bare feet and a blizzard blows down the empty highway toward them. They must wait because their feet are frozen to the ice. Amy wakes in the night and phones her brother in Fort Smith.

"I could get you in the dining room tomorrow," he says.

"I'm skilled, don't you get it?"

He sighs. "I know a woman who runs a program for kids. Lousy pay, though. And you can make good money up here, Amy."

"Talk to her."

"Those kids aren't soft like kids in the south."

"Right."

"I'll talk to her."

"Will I see the northern lights?"

"You're impractical. A bonafide flake."

"Love you, too."

Brindle leaves his Doc Martens by the door now and Amy hasn't seen his knife for days. Sometimes he slides on his wool socks down the hall with Shelagh on his back, making a sound like braying as if it hurts for him to laugh. This is how they enter the kitchen for the house meeting.

Amy hopes that Shelagh will not seduce Brindle; then she reminds herself that it's no longer her problem and besides, though Shelagh doesn't know it yet, she will be returning to her parent's home at the end of the week. Though it's months sooner than planned, the social worker sees it as the least disruptive option, made more viable because the parents have agreed that Shelagh's father will move out of the house. Brindle is going to find out that he will be given independent living, which means the ministry will support him in his own apartment on the condition he attends the training program and keeps up his psychiatric appointments. Tanis will go to a temporary foster home: placement number twenty-four.

Amy shakes salt and dribbles butter on the popcorn. She puts the bowl in the middle of the table with a large bottle of coke and four glasses. Brindle shouts at the girls to sit down and listen to Amy. From the top of the fridge Amy takes down the charts she made up two weeks before, looks them over and tosses them in the recycling bin.

She's been rehearsing all afternoon: *Shit happens. So we need to respond, not to react. Transitions are part of life. Do you know what resilient means? People move on, people you care about and you thought cared about you. Not that they didn't care about you. The really strange thing is people can care about you and move on for their own incomprehensible reasons. And sometimes the reasons are not incomprehensible. In fact, they make perfect sense. They just hurt, that's all...* she hopes she remembers it all.

Brindle insists she sit at the head of the table, the girls on one side, he on the other. He shushes them again and they turn their faces toward her. Tanis flicks her fingernail in and out of a tiny hole on the cuff of her sweatshirt. Shelagh is not wearing make-up or jewelry—her cheeks are chubby like a child's. Brindle has pushed his hair behind his ears, his eyes large and waiting.

"I'm sorry," says Amy and drops her forehead to the table with a dull thud.

After the meeting, Brindle and Tanis leave the house together without saying anything to Amy. Shelagh uses the phone in the office to talk to her mother and Amy hears her through the door, crying.

Amy is still up when Tanis arrives home at midnight.

"So you should know," Tanis says, leaning into the living room. "Brindle's been arrested. A big fucking brawl. Those guys from Esquimalt—bunch of thugs."

"Did you see it?"

"Heard about it. That's all I know. I'm going to bed."

"Tanis, are you okay?"

"Fuck, yah," she says and grins. "Why wouldn't I be?" She heads up the narrow stairwell to lie on top of her covers fully dressed for what's left of the night.

Brindle's room is in the basement in a narrow windowless walled-in space by the furnace. He wanted it that way, the privacy. There's a single bed in there, unmade, a sweatshirt and some dirty socks on the floor, one running shoe. A pile of books sit on the dresser, books about how to find a job. Amy flips through pages of photographs of young men with neat haircuts wearing button-up shirts. None of them look like Brindle. She closes the book and lays it back on the pile. Above the bed is a single poster with a graphic of an iron cross along which are images of skulls wearing top hats. Below this are the words: *Appetite for Destruction.* On the bedside table is the knife. Not realizing she'd been holding her breath, she exhales.

"Kicked a kid in the head, put him in a coma," says the social worker on the phone the next morning.

Amy sits down.

"Are you there?"

"It was a bunch of kids fighting—an accident. Tanis said... "

"It was going to happen sooner or later, knife or no knife," says the social worker.

"Where is he?"

"Juvie, but he won't be there long. They're moving him up to adult court."

Silence.

"Amy, don't even think it. You're flying out of here in a couple days, out of Brindle's life."

The night before she is to get on the plane for Edmonton, where she will transfer to a smaller plane that will take her to Fort Smith, Amy sits at the kitchen table with Tanis. It's nearly one in the morning and they are sipping hot chocolate.

"I know where she is," says Tanis.

"Shelagh?"

"The Inner Harbour."

"What's she doing down there?"

"She met a guy off one of those sailboats. You know

those big boats. Rich Americans, mostly; they dock them for a couple of nights, go up to the Empress or the Strath to the bar, or maybe for tea. Pricey, that place. Ever been to tea at the Empress?"

Amy shakes her head.

"It's stupid," says Tanis. "I went once. It's stupid."

"Is she with this guy?"

"She was shit-faced when I saw her around 10:00. They were coming down the stairs, she pawing this goof, at least 30 years old and fucking wearing a cowboy hat, what a goof, and they invite me back to his boat. I hate boats, so there's no way I'm getting on one, but I go with them to see what boat. I know what boat." She stops here and nods her head, bites her bottom lip. "I told her to get her ass home by midnight then I went to the house on Caledonia to see what was going on. There's usually a party but nothing. Something's changed. No Brindle."

The clock above the sink reads 1:15. Amy isn't tired. She's been packing all night, separating her things from Thesp's. There isn't much for Thesp to pick up after she's gone. She hadn't realized how little he'd brought with him, how much he'd already taken. "Let's go get her."

"Fuck, yah." Tanis jumps to her feet.

A half hour later at the causeway, they drop down the stairs to the harbour where boats idle along the wharves. The sea beneath them is still and soundless. In the dark, the white head of a lamp standard appears to have two outstretched arms from which hang baskets stuffed with shadowy flowers.

Amy follows Tanis along the wharf. Some of the masts are lit with tiny lights that trace skeletal sails in the blackness. Tanis stops, folds her arms across her chest and nods toward a large sailboat. There are no lights coming from within the cabin, and no one in sight. Amy listens, but hears nothing.

She pulls her coat tighter around her. "Are you sure this is it. Maybe she's gone home or... ?"

Tanis cuts her off. "Shelagh, get your ass out here. Amy's going to smack you." She leans over the boat and grabs a cushion off the deck, flings it hard at the cabin window. "Wake up you little slut right now, and get your ass out here, or Amy's coming in for you."

Amy backs down the wharf. "Tanis, come on," she says.

The door to the cabin opens, and a tall lean man, wearing only a pair of pants, steps onto the sailboat's deck. The cowboy. His pale skin gleams from his head to the waist of his pants, except for a dark tuft of hair on his chin and his chest. He looks to be a few years older than Thesp.

"What the hell," he says, and an air of authority in the voice suggests he's used to being listened to.

"You got my sister in that fancy boat of yours?" shouts Tanis.

"Go away." He bats his hand in the air, turns to go into the cabin.

Amy pulls the hood of her jacket around her face and steps forward. "You got my daughter in there?"

"Your daughter?" He swings around and peers toward Amy.

"You don't get her out here right now, I bring the cops back. Do you want to know how old she is? Idiot? Do you hear me?" Amy's heart beats fast, her fist punches the air.

"Fuck," says the cowboy, and disappears back into the cabin.

A low wail comes from behind the window. Shelagh hops from the cabin wiggling into a tiny skirt. "I didn't do nothing." Her words slur together. She throws her bra at the door of the cockpit and giggles then pulls a jacket over her bare breasts.

"Goodnight, Kid," shouts the cowboy and slams the door.

Amy holds out her hand to Shelagh.

"Amy, who invited you?" Shelagh drops spread-eagle on the deck.

Amy leaps into the boat, yanks Shelagh onto her feet and prods her onto the wharf into Tanis's hands. She and Tanis propel a whimpering Shelagh along the wharf and up the stairs to the causeway. Beneath the looming statue of Captain Cook, they release her. Shelagh wobbles on high heels then stumbles to the sidewalk, sobbing.

"She's going to bring the cops," says Tanis.

Amy grabs Shelagh hard at the shoulder and pulls her to her feet.

"Oww."

"Shelagh, bend over," says Amy.

"What? You perv." Both girls laugh.

"I said bend over." Amy is shouting.

Shelagh does as she's told, swaying a little in her drunkenness.

Amy puts her hands on her hips and swings her right leg from the knee down as hard as she can at Shelagh's buttocks. When her toe makes contact, Shelagh stumbles forward.

"A gift from Brindle," says Amy.

For a moment, Shelagh, Tanis and Amy are motionless as a tableau beneath the statue: a girl on her knees, head hung low above the sidewalk, another with crossed arms and hunched shoulders—a tall woman turned slightly on one heel, as if she might take flight.

Tanis helps Shelagh, who is quiet and shivering, to her feet. Amy walks toward the group home, weary now, with nothing to say. She's always known she cares and that she can be kind, and now she knows she can kick ass, and she can leave when she must, that all of the world's sorrow is not hers alone to shoulder and to weep over.

She hears the girls behind her, their mumbled conversation, their footsteps following her through the dark.

Exposure

Fiona watched the Jap emerge from the Willard building. Her dad said Matsubuchi thought he was better than any white man and here was the proof: his photography studio three floors above the dust and clamour of the street, a fedora topping his head and a bow tie springing from the neck of a white shirt that puffed between the lapels of a black jacket. Above polished shoes, his trousers folded into neat cuffs. Any man without coal stained into the seams of his hand was a dandy, according to her dad, and an Oriental who put on airs was worse than a dandy. Fiona didn't have a quarrel with Matsubuchi on the basis of his racial origin, and nor was she opposed to a sharp dresser with clean hands; most of the white men in Cumberland could do with a little tidying up. No, her issue with him was that he had stolen her grief; at least that's how she'd come to think of it. How he'd managed such a thing seemed a supernatural act and fear that he was a conjurer of a kind made her hesitant about approaching him.

One year ago to the day, she'd stood in her steamy kitchen squeezing Charlie's dungarees through the ringer washer, cursing the ground her husband walked on because he'd gone off to work with the tobacco. She had been looking forward to sitting on the stoop with a cigarette in the misty February morning after she'd finished the washing. Though the company forbade smoking in the mines, Charlie liked a smoke before going down and after coming up the shaft. She didn't worry about him because she married him for what she considered his indestructible nature. So when the sound of the bell calling for the draegarmen clobbered the morning's peace, and the hairs rose on her arms and a chill went through her body, she thought not of Charlie but of her dad. She pulled the plug on the washer, grabbed her coat and joined the women in the street where word had spread that the explosion was a bad one.

Later that day, the fire bosses hauled Charlie and many others from the nether regions of Mine Number Four. She didn't recognize the charred body, with skin ragged and hanging off it, as the tall hard-muscled man who'd been sleeping next to her in her dad's house for a year and a half. In the following days and months she sometimes set three places at the dinner table for her husband, her dad, and herself, half-expecting Charlie to come banging in the back stoop, black-faced and cocky with a smoke dangling from his mouth. Sometimes when she couldn't sleep, her mind got carried away on her, and she imagined Charlie was still alive, down deep in the ruined mine and not coming out because he loved that dark place better than he loved her.

Now a year after the accident it had come to this—watching the Jap from the opposite side of the street. He hesitated, adjusted his hat, and sniffed like an animal taking a measure of his surroundings. Keeping her head down so he wouldn't notice, she continued on Third and followed him along Dunsmuir until he turned into the bank. His foreign looks and gentleman airs frightened her, as if the distance between them were not a street but a chasm, strange and dangerous.

At the grocers, she picked up corned beef and a can of peas, and then walked on to the government liquor store.

She spotted Jimmy, her dad's old friend, shuffling in her direction. The stoop in his back forced him to crane his neck and he caught her eye before she could sneak past. He'd been the bartender at the Cumberland since an accident in the mine some fifteen years before. He tipped his hat and asked after her dad, exposing the dark hole of his mouth and a solitary pair of yellow teeth.

"It's like he's got knives clanging in his lungs," she said.

Jimmy shook his head. He'd lost many a good customer to Black Lung. As he spoke, his moustache bounced above his chin. "You might take him up to the hospital. They can ease the pain a little with a special breathing apparatus they got."

"I know about it and when the time comes I'll do it, but it's nowhere near time. Meanwhile he could at least leave the whiskey alone."

"Let a dying man have his pleasure, Fiona." His smile amplified the veins in his cheeks.

"It's taking food off the table, Jimmy."

He shrugged as if food was nothing compared to the need for whisky. He and some of the other men gave money to her dad and her now and then. They looked after one another that way, though funds would dry up for the widows or the kids once the men died. She turned without a word and stepped into the liquor store.

"Say hello to the old feller," Jimmy called after her.

On the way home, she felt embarrassed at how she'd stalked Matsubuchi down Dunsmuir. It was best to forget about him and besides, how could she rely on her memory from that day. The whole city had gone crazy with women wailing and sobbing in the streets—thirty-two of their men gone in one afternoon. It was like the Great War all over again, only a different kind of savagery on their very own soil. She'd left the undertaker's office in a daze, the same state she'd seen many times in other women: the stagger in the gait and the eyes as buggy as the old miners. She wouldn't have anyone around her—that hadn't changed in a year—and she didn't remember walking, how she'd gotten to the Willard Block. Her body crumbling against the building, her back braced by its cold bricks. Tears finally—rising inside of her with such force it seemed they might unhinge her very organs.

Then there had been a sound, a soft and barely audible explosion of air, which brought her back to herself and the awful scene she was making in public. When she wiped her tears, she faced a small box with a round glass window like an eye. A gentleman dressed in a black suit and shiny black shoes held the camera in his hands. He lowered his small brown eyes and bowed and before she could say anything, he disappeared around the corner of the building. It happened so quickly it might have been a dream, the kind in which a stranger sees you in your nakedness. After that day her tears dried up and ever since a steely eyed resolve pressed like stone against her days. She found it best not to think of the days gone or of those to come, only to move doggedly through the day at hand.

She walked the few blocks home through the spitting rain, opened the door to the cottage and her father's voice. "Where you been? The stove's out and I'm freezing."

He conserved his words and when he strung together more than two or three she felt bad for his suffering. He'd never been much of a talker except when he and Charlie drank and then they'd rant about the company and the union. They'd forget Fiona was even there, though sometimes when her dad wasn't looking, Charlie would slide his hand under her dress and circle her knee with his palm. If she let him, his hand would creep a little higher spreading his warmth on her skin.

It was likely a blessing Fiona's mom never met Charlie. She died when Fiona was twelve and she would have objected to his uncouth manners: chewing with his mouth open, burping after every meal. Her mom, who had not married one herself, had wanted a gentleman for her daughter. She, who'd come from England, couldn't have seen that what drew Fiona to Charlie was his promise to one day take her to his home in Ireland, away from Cumberland and back across the sea.

Fiona hung her coat at the door. "Ran into Jimmy," she said to her dad.

"Did you get the drink?" The house stank of her dad and liquor, a trace of sulphur from the stove, and the mould that grew around the windows every winter with the heavy rains.

"I'll make your dinner," she said. He was like a baby, helpless and sucking on Mama's nipple; she handed him the bottle on her way into the kitchen. She'd accepted that it would likely kill the both of them if he quit now. As uncivilized as such honesty looked, she and her father no longer pretended anything. He unscrewed the cap and swigged from the bottle's mouth. If her mother weren't already dead, such barbaric behaviour would have killed her.

In the kitchen, she shook out the ash in the stove, snapped some twigs, stuffed them through the opening, and struck a match. It wasn't like her to let the stove go out. She'd been distracted today. If her dad remembered the date, he didn't let on and she wasn't about to bring it up. She'd come to despise the cloud of black dust that rose in her face when she poured the coal into the belly of the stove, and how the flames sprung at her like prongs on the devil's fork and resolved into a slow burn that left the lingering stink of rotten eggs. When she complained, her dad would tell her to be grateful, that coal put food on her table, that if it weren't for coal's magical properties she wouldn't have her fancy stoves and washing machine, her phonograph player. He said this as if they were living the high life, her and her old dad in this rotting shack with its peeling linoleum, a motherless home with the ghost of one man lost to the mine, and another with his shredded lungs and crippled back, rhapsodizing about coal as if it were the second coming of Christ.

She fed her dad and helped him to bed, knowing she should have washed him first, but not having the energy, not tonight. She shut the door to his room, ignoring the coughing that tore at his chest.

While she did the dishes, Charlie came into her mind, pushing her to notice him, wanting to dance like they used to after her father was in bed. He was a good dancer, taught her the steps to the foxtrot. He liked the new fast jazzy music, but she liked the sad stuff about longing and loneliness and heartbreak and how it made suffering an elegant thing. He knew that and on one of his trips into Courtenay, he brought her back some Marion Harris:

> *Take me to the Land of Jazz.*
> *There is music in each breeze*
> *Even trombones grow on trees*

The words came back to her and she hugged herself and spun on her heels, imagining such a place. Dropping into a chair, she regretted that she'd sold the Victrola only a few weeks before. She'd put the money aside, told her father she'd spent it on food.

Out on the stoop in the dark, she had her last cigarette of the day. She tried to make out the shadowy shapes in the impenetrable night: the tall evergreens across the street, the house next door with a low light that pushed through a blind in a front room window. If there were any pleasure in her life, this is what it had come down to; the taste of smoke on her tongue and her mind lulled into a warmish bleak swamp. And, of course, the knowledge of a little money put aside.

Later in the tiny bedroom she'd shared with Charlie, she stood naked, shivering in front of the mirror. She had lost weight since Charlie had died. Her hipbones jutted out and her breasts were even smaller. "All a man needs is a cupful," Charlie would say. "My milk maid," he would call her, and once he said, "You're skin, it's like moonlight." He'd run his hands through her fine white-blonde hair. When they made love, his blue eyes, like a miner's lamp, would bore into hers and, afterwards, he would trace his fingers over the contours of her body as if he were drawing a sketch.

By spring, her father didn't get out of bed. The women brought casseroles and to ease his bedsores, the men came and helped turn him over. His pals sat by him and chatted idly—sometimes her father smiled between dozing—or they sat wordless, the thing they waited for hanging between them. Fiona took advantage of these times to leave the house.

One day she walked to Japtown and from the road watched the women preparing the ground for a garden. They were strong women—she often saw them hauling bags of cabbage and potatoes to the grocers—smooth-skinned, and they looked as pleased with the spring sunshine as she was herself. One of them had a sling with a baby in it looped over her shoulders. She nodded her head at Fiona and Fiona smiled. She thought the woman might be the photographer's wife, but the Orientals looked alike to her. She told herself it was the spring flowers that grew along the roadside that made her walk in that direction: lupins, goldenrod, fireweed, and yet she found herself looking for the photographer, as if she might catch him without his fine suit and with his hands in the soil. Somehow, she felt that if she could see him like that she'd concern herself less with the photograph she was certain he was coveting.

The day after her walk to Japtown, Fiona spotted an ad in the weekly posted by the photographer in which he requested a model. He specified that she must be white. He was known throughout the city for his photographs of the Orientals, and as he was the only photographer in town and, all agreed, a good one at that, he photographed the weddings of those whites who could afford him. The women speculated in hushed tones why he wanted a "white woman," and what sort of loose woman would respond to the ad.

No matter how much Fiona cleaned around her father the stink from his room hung between the walls of the house, and at night he would call out for her mother with a voice that was not a human sound. She couldn't bring herself to go to him. During the day when she walked to the grocery store, the buildings stood in sharp relief against a violent blue sky. It was as though all her senses were amplified while the normal order of her life was about to collapse. She felt panicky with a sense of urgency that couldn't be reconciled. She believed she was capable of doing any foolish thing. Fiona was the only woman in Cumberland who responded to the photographer's ad.

She wore a skirt that she had bought on her last trip to Nanaimo with Charlie. It came to her knees and clung to her hips and thighs in the new style. She remembered Charlie telling her she looked "smarty." Now, since she'd lost so much weight, it hung off her, but it felt good to get out of her mother's flowery house dresses. Her friend Irene cut her hair to just above the nape of her neck.

"You look smashing, Honey, but I don't know why you're doing it," said Irene referring not to the haircut, but to the photographer's ad.

On her way to Matsubuchi's studio, Fiona imagined the photographer looking at her through the small window of his camera, what he might see, how it would feel to have a man's eyes on her again.

She walked up three dim and stuffy flights of stairs and through a door into a room washed with so much light it gave the wooden floors a golden hue. Photographs lined the walls. Families, mostly Oriental, stood in clusters before the camera, or sat upright. She knew these to be hard working people, like the women she'd seen in the garden, most with little money, and yet they were like aristocrats before the camera, their chins up and wearing the finest clothing. She'd heard that the photographs were sent home as evidence of the good life they were leading in their new country. Closer scrutiny hinted otherwise: the slight tilt of a head as if there were a heaviness there, the light touch on a shoulder or arm as if to reassure the other that they were not alone.

She sensed that someone had stepped quietly behind her and felt the Jap's eyes on her back. She looked over her shoulder and he shifted into her line of vision. It was the first time she had seen him without his hat. Flattened against his head his black hair shone. His skin was smooth with a shade of amber, like the women in the garden. He did not wear a coat and the sleeves on his white shirt were rolled up to his elbows.

"May I help you?" No sign of recognition, his mannerisms stiff and polite.

"I've come about the ad."

He smiled. "I thought no one would come." His eyes washed quickly over her. He spoke a precise educated English.

"I need the money." She held out her hand and he took it. "I am Mrs. Braithwaite."

"I am Mr. Matsubuchi. I can explain my requirements to you, if you will be seated." He gestured toward a desk and two chairs. He settled into a chair behind the desk and waited for her to sit down. "I am perhaps an overly ambitious man and I may be faulted for learning from the coal barons. I am held in almost the same contempt, though for different reasons." He laughed and looked out the window into the sun. "But I am also an artist."

"I know nothing about art." She dug in her bag for a cigarette, but when he made no gesture of supplying her with a light or an ashtray, she thought better of it.

"It's not important." He leaned his elbow on the desk, his chin in his hand. "I only want you to model for me. It may involve two or three sittings and you must sit very still. I assume you have not modeled before."

"No. I care for a dying father and I was briefly a wife. I've not been employed otherwise."

He nodded.

"Why," she said, reaching again for a cigarette and a match, this time lighting up, "do you specify a white woman?"

"Because I know Japanese women too well and I have photographed them many times." He observed her inhaling the smoke as if he found this action interesting. His eye followed the rising smoke from the tip of her cigarette.

"Are white women so different?"

"On the surface, of course they are. The rest I will discover." He stood up.

"There is a practical reason, too. I would like to submit my work to magazines or galleries—some are taking photography now—and they are not interested in Oriental women. Take off your hat."

Her father was right—he put on airs. An artist, indeed. Still, she removed her hat slowly, shook out her new haircut. He walked around the desk, around her chair and then with a thick finger brushed a strand back from her face. She pulled away at his touch. How dare he? Indifferent to her reaction, he crouched to examine her face and neck.

She returned the next day in the early afternoon when he said the light would be best. Immediately upon her arrival, he handed her a long string of pearls and a shift of slippery pale yellow chiffon with a plunging neckline and split at the sides, so as to reveal her legs. It was a style not seen in Cumberland but seen on the likes of those in the Ziegfeld Follies. Charlie had promised that one day they would go to New York to see them live, though she'd never believed it.

"A little risqué," she said with a laugh.

"If you'd rather not, Mrs. Braithwaite."

She sighed and went behind a curtain, where she slid the dress over her head and draped the pearls around her neck. When she returned to the room, he directed her to sit on the edge of a small table facing a larger camera than the one she remembered. Perched on a tripod, it was a strange creature with a huge eye fixed on her. She sat still with the back of her head held steady in a headrest, hands folded in her lap, as though she were at peace. For each photograph— he took half a dozen—he slid a square sheet of glass in and out of the camera. Between shots, he asked her to turn her head this way and then that, to lean with her hands behind her and her front thrust forward, to smile a little but not too much. She held a mirror, and then a comb, a cigarette. She revealed a thigh, her cleavage. The light flowed into the room, and she found herself mumbling—he admonished her if she became at all animated and at times forbade her to speak—about her mother's death, her life with her father, and finally about Charlie and about how much she hated the mines, the town. She supposed what made it easy for her to talk was that he said little and yet she could feel his desire to know.

On the last day, he had her sit on a bench surrounded by pillows. She wore the same dress, but this time he'd told her to leave off the pearls. The air was cool in the studio and she shivered. He handed her a shawl, but stopped her from putting it around her shoulders. He stood close enough to her that she could smell his skin's muskiness. His eyes were hard black stones off which light refracted. He leaned close to her face and she felt that he didn't look at her but through her. She blushed and leaned away from him. He reached for the thin straps of the dress, slid them off her shoulders. He turned his back to her and went to fiddle with his glass plates.

"You have lost weight, Mrs. Braithwaite, and you are very pale. You look as if you could break in the wind. We should ask my wife to make you *nuka* and salted salmon." He spoke with his back to her.

"How would you know that I have lost weight?"

"Because of the photograph I took of you right after the mine disaster." He turned to look at her.

She pulled the straps of her dress up. "Tell me how you had the gall to take my photograph without my permission." She flushed with a long-held rage.

He bowed slightly in the manner she'd seen him do with the other businessmen in town. "It was wrong and I apologize." He sat next to her and pulled the shawl around her shoulders. "Of the few photographs I was able to get that day, it was the one of you that told the real story of the disaster. The anguish in your face, Mrs. Braithwaite. It was art."

"Art? I lost my husband. You could never understand how that feels." She got to her feet and looked down at him. "Give me my photograph now. What have you done with it? Why isn't it on the walls with your pretty families?"

"They are cowards, unlike you." She felt the weight of his hands on her shoulders. "You will see in the finished plates."

"Did you destroy the photograph?"

"I have kept it. Like a story, it was unfinished." He

turned her around to face him. He eased her on to the bench, pulled the shawl off her shoulders and looped his fingers through the straps of her dress, dropped them down. His eyes traveled over the folds of her dress to her lap and he tugged the fabric slowly up her thighs.

At first she thought to slap his hand away, but she hesitated. Next to her skin, his was golden-hued and it revived in her body, an old want. His eyes would not meet hers. He dropped his hand and returned to his camera.

At the end of the afternoon, she went home to an empty house except for Jimmy.

"He's at the hospital, Fiona. You should go, quickly."

Jimmy's face was redder than usual, his eyes puffy. He left her alone in the house for the first time in many years. She would go to the hospital in the morning. She rolled the ringer washer to the sink, washed her father's linens and hung them on the line. She opened the doors and windows, scrubbed the walls, the linoleum, and the cupboards with lye. Coal dust turned the water black and lye bleached the walls white. When she finished, beyond the tiny yard and street, the sun dropped behind the mountain in a fury of oranges and yellows. She smoked four cigarettes.

The next morning Fiona tidied up after breakfast and went directly to Matsubuchi's studio, where Matsubuchi's wife greeted her. She was not the woman Fiona had seen in the potato patch. Older and a small-boned woman, her ebony hair flipped into tiny curls at her cheekbones. She had a quick cool smile and the trace of an accent. A shift of silk clung to her tiny body with the hem gathered at her knees. They spoke of the fair weather and the coming summer.

"Will you visit our little teahouse on the lake?" Mrs. Matsubuchi said.

Two summers ago, Fiona and Irene had walked past the mines and into the trees to the Japanese teahouse on the lakeshore. There, they had sat in a makeshift pagoda with cushions on the floor beside low tables and been served by heavily made-up women in ornate kimonos with their hair piled high on their heads. The two friends had giggled at the prospect of doing housework in such get-ups. They had eaten sour pickles and dainty slices of salmon beneath paper lanterns, and sipped from tiny china cups. The women had bowed to them and Fiona saw now that it was the photographer's wife who had taken their money.

"Possibly," said Fiona, fiddling with a bracelet on her arm and glancing at her feet.

The woman turned toward Matsubuchi, who came out from his darkroom smiling and speaking in Japanese. He and his wife exchanged a few words and both laughed. Mrs. Matsubchi picked up a small handbag, bowed to Fiona and left through the door. The sound of her footsteps retreated down the stairs.

"Good morning, Mrs. Braithwaite. I am more than pleased with the plates, and I'm sure you will be, too."

He laid them out on the long table in a row.

The first one was of a woman folded into herself against a brick wall, a pretty, blonde woman with her face buried in her hands. She realized with a start that it was herself; the photograph that she had imbued with so much meaning for over a year, and yet it was an image only, a mere point in time. She laughed out loud. She did not understand what Matsubuchi saw in it.

He directed her attention to the one at the end of the row. "This one is the best," he said. In it, the body was relaxed; the eyes crinkled much like her mother's. The lips were not exactly smiling and yet they suggested a feeling of pleasure. The face was full of light and this surprised her. "She's a pretty girl, whoever she is," she said with a smile.

He nodded, watching her.

"You've tampered with it."

"A little," he said. " It doesn't mean it isn't you. It's the photographer's art to manipulate light. I would like to make one a gift to you."

She went back to the first photograph, the one of her against the wall and examined each one. She saw that he had placed them deliberately in a sequence. The grief was there, as he had said it would be and yet in each photo it seemed less. "I think you must be something of a conjurer after all," she said. She tried to explain to him how looking at her own image was somehow healing and he scoffed.

"I am a photographer, not a healer, Mrs. Braithwaite."

"Keep them all," she said. "This flesh and blood self is burdensome enough."

She went home with her pay in her purse and added it to the money she'd received for the Victrola. She sat for a long time and smoked the last of her cigarettes. If she went to the hospital, she might lose her nerve. She gathered most of her belongings into a single trunk and she was on the late train to Union Bay, where she had booked a hotel room for one night. What else was she to do? In a few hours her father would be dead if he wasn't already, and all of her known family gone. She came from parents who went elsewhere and she suspected it was in her blood to do the same. At 4:00 am the following day she embarked on the S.S. Princess Mary for Victoria. On the deck, she filled her lungs with the sea's clean-flowing breezes and with her eyes followed the sun's sparkle on the water's wide surface. A hazy line in the distance marked the horizon. She felt for the first time what it might be like to be a miner—at the end of the day rising from the dark into the light.

She had never been to Victoria though her mother had spoken fondly of it: said it was a fanciful place with streets lined in flowers and all manner of dandies. In reality, she was certain it was a place like any other with its dirt and its meanness, but one in which she might at least imagine herself into a finer life.

On the Heron's Watch

Three weeks ago, Sharon picked up her cellphone and heard Kev's voice for the first time in eight years. He'd gotten her number through an old friend. Sharon's mother wouldn't give it to him.

"I've been sober for six months now," he said.

Words broke in her throat. She swallowed. "That's good," was all she could say. Then when she collected herself, "Grandpa died."

"The old guy is gone?"

"He left me the cabin in Fanny Bay."

"No kidding." Kev laughed. "Still lots of oysters?"

"Oh yah. And dry rot, mould. Rats. But we got rid of them. The roof leaks." She wished he could see her smile. "Trina and I are living here."

"Seriously?"

"Yes."

"You're crazy."

"*We love it, Kev, and it's where a kid should be, close to the water. We're going to fix it up.*"

"You and whose army?"

"I'll figure it out."

He was quiet for so long she thought he had hung up. She hoped he'd hung up and she hoped he hadn't hung up

"I could help you," he said.

And here he was, four days later. Cloud cover cast a bone-white light across the beach where he crouched next to Trina, elbows on his knees, shoulders hunched against the wind, a tremor beneath his skin. That was new. Sharon put it down to the drink that had fueled him those years in the oilsands. He was like a man come home from war, her husband.

Kev picked up an empty oyster shell, hinged it open then closed, making his voice shrill. "Help me, help me. Let me out. Let me out."

Trina giggled and glanced at him, resisting a smile. She went back to uncovering rocks, poking at tiny crabs then tilted her head toward him. "My mom and I have derbies with the crabs. Mine win." She caught a strand of hair in her mouth and stuck out her bottom lip.

Kev stood. The grey sky met the grey sea, and on the horizon the light shimmered like silver. Sharon stepped beside him.

"She looks like me," he said.

"What did you expect?"

Still as a heron, he watched the ocean and watched his daughter. Minutes later, Trina jumped to her feet and wandered toward the tideline where she scooped oysters into the basket she made of her jacket. She ran back and dropped them with a bang into the bottom of the steel bucket. He picked the bucket up and followed her. Sharon hollered instructions on how to choose the best ones: small but not too small and covered in the least amount of barnacles. She left them to it and sat on a flat drift of shale. Out beyond the low wire fence that marked the oyster lease, the edge of the water idled with the dithering wind. The centre of Baynes Sound dropped from a shale shelf that made up the beach at low tide, blackened with the mud of centuries. Further up, where shale crumbled to sand and gravel, bladder wrack and a pile of driftwood littered the shore beneath the high bank. Above, a row of tall firs dwarfed the cabin.

Trina and Kev raced down the beach, Trina giggling and Kev making a show of gasping. Kev dropped onto the beach beside where Sharon sat and Trina fell onto her mother's lap. A flock of surf scoters lifted off the water and skimmed frantically along its surface, their cries a high-pitched staccato. Then for a few seconds, all noise subsided. And a heron's wings bellowed the air as it rose and departed.

The stairs to the cabin were soft with rot. Sharon took Trina's hand. The air was needled with the smell of cedar. "I forgot to tell you, I ran into Ricky yesterday."

Kev glanced at her. "He's still around."

"Oh, yah. Cowboy Rick."

"Do the women still love him?"

"It's his limp they love. He gets away with acting like a buffoon because of it."

"Have you no pity?"

"I wouldn't be stupid enough to mistake pity for love." She walked ahead of him.

"Why'd you tell him I was here?"

"Maybe he could get you a job."

"A job?" Behind her, he hesitated. "Is he still working in the bush?"

"Nobody is these days."

Later, Sharon yanked the sheets and the bedding from the couch, shook out the blanket and passed one end to Trina.

"Kev says pit bulls are good watch dogs." Trina was dog-crazy these days: stuffed dogs and stickers, books from the library on dog breeds, sketched dogs on her homework.

"I'm scared of them," said Sharon. She finished folding

the blanket and sheets, fluffed a pillow and carried the pile of bedding to the hall closet. Trina prattled at her heels.

"Where did you meet him?"

"High school, I told you," said Sharon.

"Was he your boyfriend?"

"For me to know and you to find out." Sharon closed the closet door, grabbed her daughter, spun her around and squeezed her hard. "I'll let you go if you never mention a pit bull again."

Trina shrieked and pushed away from her mother. "I'm never going to have a boyfriend," she shouted and banged out the front door.

Two years after Kev left, Cam moved in. Trina was three. Everyone said he'd be a good father to Trina. He didn't drink and had a steady job in maintenance at the school board. He was something Kev could never be, something Sharon thought she needed. Trina was three and a half when she told him to move out, and Sharon's mother didn't speak to Sharon for two months.

Kev opened the kitchen door, bringing in the cool air off the water. "You need a new roof, Sharon."

"It's that bad."

"Shingles broken and missing. I can see the plywood in places. Moss hasn't been scraped for years." He stepped inside and shut the door, slipped off his boots.

"How much will it cost?"

"Ten thousand, about. I don't know if it's worth it." He went to the sink and washed his hands. "You should build."

"With what?"

He wiped his hands on the dishtowel and shrugged.

After lunch, she drove Trina into town for a sleepover at Mandy's. When she returned, Ricky's truck was in the yard. A cloud of cigarette smoke met her as she opened the door. Kev and Ricky sat at the kitchen table, the empty soup tin serving as an ashtray between them. A six-pack of Lucky Lager held together by a strip of plastic sat in front of Ricky. One can open in Ricky's hand, and Kev sipping from a coffee cup. Without taking off her coat, she went to the sink and pushed open the kitchen window. Outside a slight breeze wrinkled the surface of the ocean.

Kev butted his cigarette. "Hey, Ricky, Sharon doesn't like smoking in the house."

Ricky glanced at Kev then at Sharon, then butted his cigarette. The baseball cap on his head said *Blink if You Want Me*. After tipping the can of beer into his mouth, he wiped his lips with the back of his sleeve.

Sharon hung her coat on the hook by the door and poured herself a coffee. "Want more?" she asked Kev.

"Sure." Holding her eyes, he passed his cup. She swirled the sugary remains and sniffed: coffee. He continued to watch her.

"It's cold for April," she said, turning from him. She'd forgotten the state of vigilance in which she once lived with him: the necessary sharpness of the sense organs. The violation she committed with all her watching.

"Decent coin in McMurray, eh?" said Ricky.

"Things are expensive."

"What kind of things, Dude?" Ricky leaned across the table, his cheeks inflated to tiny balloons.

"Rent, for example." Kev reached for the cup Sharon passed him. The cuffs on his sweater were frayed. She might repair that for him. She sat in the chair between him and Ricky.

"Where you working, Buddy?" asked Kev.

"Oyster lease over on Denman." Ricky sipped his beer, gestured toward the window and across the sound to the island.

"Hard work?"

Ricky shrugged. "If it's cold, you know, you can freeze

your ass off on the boat. Not minus thirty like the rigs, nothing like that." As if Ricky would know, as if he'd ever lived anywhere but the valley. He tipped the can of beer to his mouth, drained it, and hesitated. "You're not telling me you're interested, are you?"

"Maybe."

"It's pussy work, Kev. Pardon me, Sharon. And the pay's the shits. They're putting in a coal mine. You heard about that, hey Sharon. Decent pay. That's the job for you and me, Buddy."

"I don't believe they'll do it, Rick." Sharon stood up and took the bowl of oysters from the fridge, dropped it and a shucking knife on the table between the two men.

"Why wouldn't they?" said Ricky, sliding the knife between the two valves in one deft movement.

"You're good," said Kev.

"What? Oh, this." Ricky poured the oyster into his mouth, shoved the bowl across the table to Kev. He handed him the knife.

Kev picked up an oyster and repeated what Ricky had done, but he pushed too hard; the shell cracked and the knife slipped into the flesh of his finger. He jerked it away and blood bubbled from a small cut.

Ricky hooted while Sharon sprang to her feet. She grabbed a paper towel and passed it to Kev. "Ricky is the oyster shucking champ around here, Kev."

Ricky snorted and snapped the tab back on another beer, swigged, then pried open an oyster and held it up for Kev. "For you, Bro."

Kev tipped the fleshy grey mound into his mouth and swallowed. "Brings me back."

Sharon took Kev's hand into her own. She paused, holding it there. It was almost twice the size of hers, and his fingernails were bitten from a nervous habit he hadn't lost. She removed the bloody paper towel and bandaged his finger. He caught her eye and laced his fingers through hers. She pulled her hand away.

Ricky separated an oyster for her, but she shook her head. "You must miss your grandpa, Sharon. I liked running in to him down there at the dock. He always wanted to show me the latest thing he was doing on his boat. He was gold."

"Everyone liked him."

"Guess you lost your fishing buddy, hey Kev." Ricky leaned back in his chair.

"That was a few years back."

"Remember that twenty-five pounder? A spring. They still got that picture up in the pub."

Kev nodded and smiled. She could tell it pleased him. His family had come to the valley with the air force, his father a mean whisky-soaked flight lieutenant. Sharon wasn't there to see it, but Kev told her that one time he saw her grandfather, who was half his father's size, fling Kev's drunken father over his shoulder and drop him off the end of the dock. When her grandfather was dying she asked him about the incident. In an uncharacteristic burst of acrimony, the old man said that he had few regrets, but one was that he hadn't drowned the son-of-a-bitch. At seventeen, Kev stayed on when his father was transferred to Cold Lake. He wanted to be part of the valley. He wanted to be with her.

Ricky dumped the last of his beer into his mouth. "Did you fish at MacMurray?"

Kev cleared his throat and shifted. "A little."

"What do you catch out there?"

"Oh, you know. Freshwater: Whitefish, mostly."

"Good?"

Kev shrugged. "I prefer salmon."

"I'll leave you guys to it," said Sharon, pushing herself up from her chair. She slipped on her boots and jacket. On her way out the door, she heard Ricky say, "When we get that mine, hell, it'll be good as Fort Mac around here, better, even."

As she closed the door, one of them, Ricky or Kev, tapped a beer can with a fingernail: the ping of metal.

The sun filtered through a thin layer of cloud, splaying out into a silvery fan. The water's surface undulated like a bolt of silk. Sharon liked it best this way, imagining the wind spent and resting around some headland. She settled on her favourite sitting rock, a daily ritual.

Close to a year ago now, all that was left of their family— her mother, Trina, and Sharon—had scattered her grandfather's ashes on this beach. They stood at the tide line and took handfuls of his remains from the box the funeral parlour gave them. The tide had been on its way out and a south-easterly blew up the sound. The wind tore the cries of gulls from their throats, shredding them above the white-capped sea. The ashes, heavy with traces of bone, fell with a splash and it was only the finer ash, the flesh and sinew, the wind stole away. Now she imagined her grandfather in the pitch and roll of the water. Her mother believed that his spirit protected Sharon, his only grandchild. This belief was the extent of any religion in their lives.

Hands across her eyes startled her out of her thoughts. She jumped to her feet and screamed while Kev caught her around the waist then rested his chin on her shoulder. It was the closest he'd been to her since his arrival four days before. She heard Ricky's truck spit gravel in the driveway.

"He's gone," he said, smiling. She could smell his breath: coffee and cigarettes, and also the familiar outdoor smell of him; it hadn't changed in all those years. Without letting go, he eased her back onto the rock, stretching his legs out on either side of her, and she leaned against his chest. They sat, only commenting on the light as it shifted down into dark, until a chill rose into the air.

Later that night, she lay next to him in her bed, the dark and the silence all around them. At the cabin, the silence got inside of her as if it were an element, like oxygen. She'd started to breathe it.

"What was it like in Murray?" She wanted to know what kept him from her and Trina.

"Cold," he said.

"I know that."

"I mean really cold. I got frostbite a few times, almost lost my toes and my fingers."

She wrapped her arm around his waist and held him closer. "Tell me more."

He rolled on to his side, facing away from her. "You work all the time, that's all. But a lot of people do that these days."

"Not me. Trina comes first." Sharon sighed and put her hands behind her head. She worked part-time as a daycare assistant.

"You're too good for words, Sharon."

"People say that and it's not true. I hate Ricky and he's a cripple; I think my boss is a bitch: and if you really must know, there's this guy, a father who drops his son off at the daycare. He's married which makes him all the more attractive. Good fathers and good husbands are sexy."

Her words flopped in the silence like a caught fish. She faced his back. She would ruin things. She wrapped her arms around his waist, touched cheek to backbone. "Trina and I saw on the news these ducks that drowned on the tailing ponds. It made Trina cry. I know it sounds crazy, but as soon as they said it was near Fort McMurray, I thought maybe you'd be walking by or something—that I'd see you."

She recalled the image of a duck turned a glossy black struggling to escape the sludge, looking more like a creature bubbling up from below than a bird descended from the blue sky. The newsman said the ducks had been fooled; that they had seen what they thought was a lake and landed in the oil's waste.

She thought he'd gone to sleep so his voice in the dark was a surprise. "Last summer me and my buddy, Stu, went fishing on the Athabasca. Pissed up, beer cans rolling around the bottom of the boat. I'm not proud of it." He flipped onto his back. "But the air was sweet that morning. No smell of oil. It reminded me of here, so clean. I thought of fishing with the old guy, the salmon. Stu and I caught three Whitefish. They had these big sores and lumps on them and were all streaked with blood. Stu wanted to eat them. Big talk, you know, like it would make him a big man. Fucking idiot." He turned back to her. "I couldn't drink after that."

She woke late the next morning. He and his truck were gone. She showered and made coffee, got out the vacuum cleaner, sighed, and instead threw on her boots. Her grandfather had told her, "Touch your boots to the shore everyday." The sky was that high overcast that comes before a shift in the weather: the water calm, expectant. She picked up a stick and tossed it into the sea. It startled a heron, sent him squacking skyward.

She was vacuuming when Kev walked in the house around noon.

"Where were you?" She didn't mean for her voice to sound so shrill.

"Whoa." He reached for her and she stepped back.

He dropped his hands to his side. "An AA meeting and I stopped at the hardware store on the way back."

He'd bought tar to mend the roof and caulking for around the bathtub. He showed her how to remove the mouldy strip and apply the clean stuff; how to seal the windows from the cold. He went back up on the roof and they worked until Mandy's mom dropped off Trina. They made pizzas that night and watched "My Little Pony" with Trina.

The days unfolded with Sharon driving Trina to school and then going to work at the daycare centre until noon. When she got back to the house, she made lunch for herself and Kev. They talked about rotted siding and the price of lumber, how he had trouble getting the insulation in under the floor. He chopped wood and repaired the stairs to the beach. He painted the living room. He called Ricky twice and Ricky said, "A couple more weeks, something will come up." After his AA meetings, Kev checked the Employment Services office.

It took Sharon back to an earlier time before he went away, how she'd count the hours of his sobriety, cherish them like a drowning woman who'd found dry land.

Three weeks later, waiting for Trina to finish her swim class at the recreation centre in town, she read a notice. It was about a meeting at the Fanny Bay Hall where a mining company executive and a representative from an environmental group were going to talk about the proposed coal mine. All the way home, while Trina chattered about her swim lesson and her friends, Sharon thought about the place where they wanted to put the coal mine up the mountain a few kilometres from the cabin. She imagined the rivers falling from the snowfields and the melting glacier, falling freely and cleanly through the trees into the welcoming sea. And the mouths of the rivers receiving the salmon in the fall after their long journey home. It was the falling she felt, as if she were dissolving into the ocean, becoming water. It's what she longed for, yet you couldn't raise a child this way, repair an old house, stop a coal mine.

When she got home after work, Ricky's truck was in the drive. He and Kev stood on the bank facing the beach with their backs to her. Ricky leaned on a wooden cane, one he'd carved himself with the head of a snake for his hand-hold. A cigarette dangled from Kev's mouth. Trina went into the house and Sharon stopped beneath the cedar. The heron stood on the beach, one leg raised, waiting. The wind pushed hard against the tide, but she could hear Ricky's voice.

"Three hundred jobs at eighty-thousand a year and the fucking tree huggers are trying to stop it."

"What about the oysters?" She had to strain to hear Kev's voice. Ricky's was louder.

"Nothing's going to happen to the oysters. We'll buy them from China if we have to. Christ, Kev, this is the best news this valley has had in a long time."

Kev stepped closer to the bank and sucked on his cigarette.

"Jesus, Kev. Look at the dump you live in. I mean Sharon's sweet, but get real, Bro. This isn't you."

Sharon crossed the yard in a half dozen quick strides. "Go Ricky."

"Sharon, I didn't... "

"I mean it. Leave my place right now."

Ricky held his hands palm up. "Chill, Sharon. I'm out of here."

When he'd gone, Kev dropped his cigarette and ground it into the dirt with his foot. "That was an over-reaction."

"Really."

His gaze remained on the sea.

"I'll make dinner," she said.

"Sharon." He didn't move. "We've got to pull out that wall in the bathroom and I don't have any money left."

She faced his back. "We'll live with it until you get work." She went into the house and left him standing there.

A few minutes later she heard his truck leave the driveway. At midnight, she was dozing on the couch when her phone rang.

His voice was slurred. "You've seen nothing until you've seen a refinery lit up on a winter night. It's a thing of beauty, Baby."

"Come home when you're sober, Kev." She hung up.

He came home the next night, just as she and Trina sat down to dinner. Trina jumped up and grabbed him a plate from the cupboard.

"No thank you," he said, waving his hand.

He walked through the kitchen to the bathroom. Sharon heard the shower and continued eating. She kept her eyes on her plate. She heard his electric razor. While Trina cleared the table, she pulled the blankets from the closet and tossed them on the couch. He came from the bathroom in his housecoat, his hair slick to his head. He saw the blankets and, without saying anything, curled beneath them, his long body occupying the whole of the couch. He was asleep within minutes.

Sharon sat at the kitchen table helping Trina with her homework. There was no separation between the living room and the kitchen in the tiny cabin, so Sharon was conscious of his breath, and when he moved, the sound of the weight of him on her couch. After they finished homework, Sharon made Trina some herbal tea to take into her room.

Trina stood on the rug in her bedroom, hands by her side. "Am I like him, Mommy?"

Sharon shook her head and placed the tea on the dresser. "How about we get ourselves one of Mandy's puppies? A nice little mutt. We don't need a pit bull." She kissed Trina goodnight and went to bed alone.

The next day she arrived home from work and found him on the beach seated on a log examining an empty oyster shell. The clouds were low, not raining, but weeping moisture. She laid her hand on his shoulder and his t-shirt was damp. His arms were goose-pimpled from the cold. She had forgotten how he would punish himself.

"The coal mine meeting is at the hall tonight."

"You go." He stared into the empty shell.

Later, she came home with a sign and pounded it in at the head of the driveway before she came into the house. *No Coal Mine.*

A week later, he called from St. John's on the other side of the country. They were flying him out the next morning. The rig was one hundred kilometres offshore.

"I'll send money," he said, his voice so distant she had to ask him to repeat himself.

She stood at the window. Out on the beach, the heron lifted its primeval body from a pile of shale, spread its wings and vanished down the shore.

Paddling Against the Ferryman

Rita's brother, Rodney, should be here. She imagines him in a kayak sliding into the trough of the swell before her, disappearing then re-appearing, his paddle a black wing and his body half-buried in the boat.

A half hour later, she and her husband, Daryl, land on tiny Vargas Island. Clouds drizzle a prickly rain and the shoreline reeks from the rot of low tide. A giant of a woman in red rubber boots stands beneath the firs at the top of the bank with her arms outstretched. Tsonqua, thinks Rita, who's seen the Wild Woman mask at the museum.

"Welcome to paradise," says the woman. She introduces herself as Stel. For Stella, for stealth.

Rita uncurls her legs from inside the kayak and hoists herself out of the cockpit. Rodney would hate the indignities of the exit. She stinks of neoprene and sweat and it is as though her hips are seized in a vice grip. She and Daryl follow Stel up the bank where a faux Tudor building pops into view from between the trees and the low-hanging fog. Underfoot, the stairs to the front door are soft with damp and rot.

Their room is only big enough to accommodate the bed and a bedside table. A bulb in the ceiling casts a sickly light and there's a hint of mould in the air. Daryl goes for a shower, and Rita lays on her back on the bed with her legs up the wall. She reaches for her cellphone and texts her son.

We made it safe. Are you home?
Watching TV.
Sarah?
Dunno
Behave and text if Sarah not home by 10. Love you
TTFN

Rita tucks her hands under her head and closes her eyes. Rodney would hate it: the mould and the chill in the air. He likes luxury.

Last summer at the cabin she'd stepped onto the deck and paused behind the Adirondack where Rodney sat. In the dusk, his body was a bolt of fabric draped over the chair's seat, ready to slide at any moment. He'd lost weight. It was rare—this opportunity to look at him without him knowing and to see him so still. Usually everything about Rodney from his limbs to his tongue was in motion, so that it was hard to get a fix on him. He stared at the shadowy mountain across the lake. She cleared her throat and offered him a glass of wine. He took it from her while she settled into the chair next to him.

"You hiding out here?" Rita asked.

"Avoiding bedtime stories. Don't tell my nephews or Mia."

"You're such a fake."

He laughed. "You and me are the same."

"It's board games I hate, not bedtime stories."

"Not Monopoly again."

"Blame it on my daughter. Where'd I go wrong?"

"You didn't go wrong."

This near-compliment was not like him who was always quick with the wisecracks. It's how she and he communicated. Not this. "How's that possible... you know, not to screw up my kid's lives, not so far, anyway?" she asked.

He shrugged. "I'm sure you have in some way that hasn't shown up yet, so relax."

She smacked his arm.

He grunted and flung his hands in the air. "No good fights around here anymore? Couldn't we ply Mom with alcohol—she's not drinking enough these days—tell Mia I believe in adult-only gated communities, call dad a homophobic asshole for old time's sake. Couldn't we, huh?"

"You bored?"

"A little."

"How long you going to stay this time?"

"You have no faith in me." His voice dropped to the level of the wind that stirred on the surface of the lake.

"It's too quiet here, Rod, I mean compared to Toronto."

"I love it, especially, here. I mean, here at the lake. I feel safe. I can see land on the other side. If you think about it, it's not much different than Toronto, really, except there's trees instead of buildings, and you know, traffic noise and people, lots of strangers in Toronto, theatres and interesting stores, art galleries or bars with attractive men. No, there's none of that. The lake, yes, I love this lake."

Rodney's words trailed off as if caught on the wind, and there was a pause before Rita spoke. A chill rose from the lake, and she hugged her sweater to her chest. "You used to love the ocean. Remember, swimming off Tofino in those big waves, so cold our skin went numb, Mom yelling at us to get out before we froze to death."

"We'd come out and go back in before we even stopped shaking." He mimicked their childhood trembling, his body in spasms. But he appeared grotesque, so she couldn't laugh like she knew he wanted her to.

He fell still again and they sat in darkness. After a few minutes, his voice startled her. "You guys go back to Victoria. Leave me here for awhile."

.A week later he called Rita one night, his voice rapid fire. "It smells like swamp here and I'm going to rot to death. Everyone in Toronto dreams of living on the west coast, the operative word being, *coast*. What am I doing hiding in this mouldy cabin in this stinking valley surrounded by rednecks when the seaside is a few kilometres away?" It was in his nature, this heightened awareness of shorelines and trees, buildings and streets, the particular kinds of walls a place imposed on him.

"Where to now?" she asked.

"Tofino."

"Are you sure?"

"I'll get a job in a resort. They have tons of them. People come from all over the world. The waves come all the way from Japan. The beach is spectacular."

"You really want to wait tables or work the bar? When did you last have a job, any job?"

"I've been busy with school and things. Don't be a bitch, big sister."

"How's your health, Rod?"

"Elvis hasn't left the building, if that's what you're asking." He hung up.

In many ways, he was the same as ever and this put her mind at ease.

In the dank room on Vargas Island, Rita rolls onto her side and pulls a blanket over herself. Rodney would have had to work too hard on the crossing. He'd only kayaked once before on Lake Ontario and it wasn't as dangerous there as on the west coast. He preferred the sun and sandy beaches. When he was younger, he'd sent her postcards from Mexico and in the last few years, digital photos and emails. Sometimes, after a few glasses of Pinot Noir he'd strut across the living room mimicking himself with a "big ass camera" hanging around his neck. He'd hold the invisible camera near his crotch and wiggle his hips. You couldn't help but laugh. Then he'd sit down and get quiet, tell her about some little kid who wanted money and had sores on her arms, how he'd walked right by and pulled out his hand cleanser. How bad he felt.

Daryl comes back from the shower rubbing his head with a towel. He pulls on jeans, a t-shirt, and a fleece jacket. He looks good for his age, ruddiest in the outdoors, competent in a kayak.

"Let's go downstairs," he says.

"I'm tired."

"I'm hungry."

She gesturs to a bag of chips.

He sits on the bed. "What's up?"

"I don't feel social."

He sighs and gets to his feet.

"Mia says Rodney's got the flu," she says, recalling a conversation with her sister the night before.

"So, he could have phoned you and told you he wasn't feeling well."

"I shouldn't have kicked him out of our house."

"I thought this was our holiday. It's like he's here even though he's not."

"Tell me he deserved it."

"You've both got tempers."

"Are you taking his side?"

"He needled you. He loves the drama, the explosion. We've been over this." With a shiver, Daryl zips up his coat.

"No one likes the drama, Daryl. People say that and it's not true. It's painful, the drama."

He leans towards her, rubs her neck.

She wants to leave it: Rodney and work and the kids, to leave it back on Vancouver Island.

The next day Rita sinks into a nest of cushions on the couch in front of a stone fireplace that dominates one wall in the lobby. Outside, Fletch, the guide from Kayak Adventure Tours, paces the slippery rocks in front of the window. Hooded in Gortex, all muscle and crewcut, he's restless as a weathervane in the fierceness of the storm that makes paddling impossible that day. She flips open a book Rodney had pressed on her: *Powering Up Your Happiness Quotient*. He's changed. Years ago, it was *Become a Millionaire in Six Short Weeks*. Since he's returned from Toronto it's a bottle of wine a night and when he comes to her house, she drinks along with him and it's two bottles of wine.

"Your liver?" she said once.

"My liver is my business."

She has googled *AZT and liver damage*, read three lines and closed the link.

Stel's husband, Charlie, shuffles into the living room and drops an armful of wood on the hearth. He crouches before the fire, stirs the flames, and adds a log. His chiseled face looks carved from stone, centuries-old. They've never actually been introduced. It feels unnecessary, as he seems barely there and yet ubiquitous, skulking always at the backside of furniture, bent and quiet.

Log out of those negative thought patterns, Rita reads. She could kill Rodney for not being there, however uncharacteristic his enthusiasm for an outdoor sport had seemed.

"Why so upset about this trip?" Daryl had asked. "It's not like it's the first time Rod has bailed."

She snaps the book shut just as Stel drops on the couch beside her.

Stel holds a dusty wine decanter in one hand, and two glass tumblers in the other. "Empty our cellars," she says, her voice ballooning into the room. She pours a burgundy liquid smarmy with the scent of rancid fruit then offers a glass to Rita. "Charlie says it's too soon, that the grape hasn't set. He's all in a pout again, but I say there could be a tsunami today, and then what, all our labour for naught." Cherry red lipstick smudges the crease above her upper lip. Stel's skin stretches over the frame of her skeleton, how Rodney has started to look.

Rita hesitates and Stel gazes at her, a watery-eyed boozy gaze.

"You want me to drink first. That's wise. One must keep oneself safe from dangers of storms, locusts and poison—a lot of work, this keeping oneself alive." She gulps the wine, licks her lips and refills her glass. "We don't get much company," she says. "Not this time of year, anyway. I prefer it that way, actually."

Rita sips from her glass. The wine slivers down her throat into her gut, settles in a blast of heat.

"What happened to the other member of your party?" asks Stel.

"You didn't get my message? I left it on your phone to say my brother wouldn't be coming."

"I did get it. I mean, what happened? Why isn't he here? Is he ill?"

"Yes; I mean no, not exactly."

Stel gives the impression she might dissolve any minute into the grey light. Her breath is a cool draft of damp earth, and her body, dank-smelling like the lodge, looks as though she's grown from the building itself, sprouted between its cracks. "I don't mean to pry," she says. "It comes from living on this tiny bit of land in the middle of the sea. Washed up like so many drift logs, loosed of all manners and conventions."

"Have you been here long?"

"For twenty years and only off the island three times in all those years."

"How do you manage?"

"Charlie goes across to Tofino with my lists."

"Do you ever get lonely?"

"We have guests, like yourself, not so much in the winter, but all summer, and I ply them with questions about the outside world, though truthfully, I'm no longer interested, so you'll be spared. I'm more interested in what people bring here. I can see it written all over their faces, what they can't leave behind. You get attuned to those sorts of things in a place like this." She flashes an open-mouthed smile at Rita. "Besides, I have my hobby. Would you like to see?" She stands, goes over to the mantle and lifts an object from amongst a clutter of seashells, magazines and a wooden clock. So odd is the object, Rita is surprised she hasn't noticed it before.

Stella places it on the middle cushion of the couch where it wobbles like a small creature. Twisted driftwood of varying thickness thrust upward and outward as if reaching for something; branches of a miniature tree or the tendrils of a sea-creature. From these hang broken bits of shell and flattened plastic, shards of tin cans, blunted glass, the fractured iconic script of Coca-Cola on tin, a torn shoe with its sole missing and from the highest branch dangles a large rusted fish hook.

"This is the junk of towns, the debris, the flotsam, the jetsam. The remains. I have many more of these. Sometimes Charlie takes them into Tofino, and they sell them in the tourist shops." She laughs and sips her wine, lights a cigarette.

That night Rita dreams that Rodney washes up on the island strapped to a cross made of driftwood.

The next morning Rita spots moonsnails beneath her kayak, smooth with nipples that make them look like women's breasts. Rodney would have laughed and wanted to reach for them.

"You're drifting," shouts Daryl, who paddles with the

rest of the group a few metres ahead. He turns his boat and slides across the water next to her. "Paddle from your core." He thrusts one end of the paddle deep into the water and twists his body to drag it behind him then forward again and low across the bow. There's a rhythm in it, one she isn't able to achieve.

A few minutes later, they catch up to the group. Fletch has rafted everyone together into a flotilla, its bright colours aberrant under the high cloud cover, on the gray sea. As they come alongside the boats on the outside, Fletch, with the steely eye of a general, cuts his gaze in Daryl and Rita's direction.

"Kayaking is like any sport." He swings his paddle in the air and addresses the group. "You are in charge. The ocean may be bigger than you, but you are in control."

For a time they paddle along the shore. Bat stars and sea anemones blossom on the rocks. Rita allows herself to drift. When they were kids, she and Rodney collected starfish, gave them voices as if they were human, then left them to die.

Daryl tells her to keep paddling.

A woman capsizes. First she is there, then she is gone. Fletch and another man speed to her side and spin the kayak upright as if it were a toy. The woman, to show she is a good sport, laughs, but later she shivers so badly Fletch jams his toque on her head, then shouts that it's time for lunch. When they beach on Meares Island, he orders the woman to change and drink something hot. The woman scurries into the trees with a bundle of dry clothes.

After lunch, all but Fletch hike across the island between the biggest cedars Rita has ever seen. She strains her neck to look upward along the massive trunks through the bough-laced canopy.

"One thousand years old." Daryl's voice is a whisper at her side.

"When will they die?" she asks.

Daryl shakes his head and takes her hand while still looking upward. "Another five hundred years, maybe." The kayaks are down on the beach in a neat row, sterns above the tideline. Fletch has remained there and Rita imagines him pacing in the rising wind.

Back on the water, whitecaps slash the ocean's surface and it's difficult to pinpoint the direction of the wind. Rita and Daryl raft together, their paddles across one another's hulls. They hang back as the group departs amidst Fletch's frantic instructions.

"Remember the ferry line," says Daryl. "We trick the wind by paddling into it. Not straight across, but on an angle that overshoots our destination. And the wind pushes us home." He smiles and releases her boat. "Don't stop paddling."

Rita arches forward taking the kayak on the angle that Daryl set for them. Behind her, he hollers encouragement. Push into the wind. All her strength and the waves coming from every direction   Paddle from your core   smacking the bow   shock of icy water stinging her eyes and her tongue salty tasting wind whipping spray into her face   tears flying off her cheeks   Remember the ferry line   whorl of wind and sound of water inside her ears   Don't stop paddling Not strength but technique   Push into the wind   Angle into the wind   Don't stop paddling Home Refuge Home How she'd let him down   How she'd failed him   wet nose running   The sea going off in every direction   tears and more tears flying off in every direction   How she'd let him down Don't stop paddling Don't stop   Don't Don't Don't die Don't die

Don't die.

When she and Daryl beach, the other kayaks are already there. She drops the paddle, scrambles up the bank and into the lodge. From the living room they holler as she squishes up the stairs in neoprene boots, spray skirt dripping on the carpet leaving a trail of sea water behind her.

Stel stands at the top of the stairs, gray hair loose and electrified, eyes sunk deep into their sockets. Like Rodney's eyes. "Your cellphone, Dear. It's been ringing all day." Rita pushes past her into the room.

She grabs the phone. "I'm here," she says.

"Finally." Mia's voice.

"I just got back to the lodge."

"Where are you?"

"Kayaking. You knew that."

"Right. It's Rodney."

"I know."

"You do?"

"I felt something."

"It was sudden."

"It's been twenty five years, Mia."

"I mean—the hemoglobin count falling—when can you get back?"

"We were headed back the day after tomorrow."

"Don't wait until then."

She nestles the cellphone between ear and shoulder, rubs her chilled hands.

Early morning fog swirls around Charlie on the beach. He'd loaded their kayaks onto the skiff. A chill rises off the water. Rita picks her way down the bank toward him, soil and rock collapsing beneath her feet. Halfway down, an arbutus leans hard across the path toward the sea. She ducks under it, and slides on loose stones the last few metres to the shore. Fog conceals the mainland, forty-five minutes across the channel.

"Godspeed." A woman's voice descends from the bank where Stel waves in the mist outside the door of the lodge. Rita waves back.

Charlie pulls the bow of the skiff into the water. He gestures for Rita and Daryl to jump in, and they scramble onto the metal bench. Shivering, she shoves a toque on her head, over which she snaps the hood of her raincoat.

"It'll be warmer when the fog lifts," says Daryl. She'd told him to stay, come back with the others, but he wouldn't hear of it. As Charlie pushed out and climbed in, the boat shook. Nothing about the morning was steady. On the other side, it was five hours to Victoria from Tofino. Around three hundred kilometres. *Godspeed*: how fast was that?

Charlie guides the boat through a barrier of bone-white fog. In a few metres she can see on either side, the ocean glints silver, crinkled like paint after an application of remover. A soundless world, but for the sputtering of the engine. She watches Charlie scan the visible surface. What obstacles does he imagine concealed in the fog? How many times and in what conditions has he crossed the channel?

One month before, Rita had cleared out the spare room in the basement, filling two boxes with stuff the family had outgrown or forgotten. A few days later, Rodney moved in and she told Daryl it would only be until he got on his feet. Soon, the house smelled like bleach after Rodney's cleaning episodes. He scrubbed the downstairs bathroom, the kitchen counters, anything he touched. He washed his clothes twice a day, showered twice a day. Once he brought home tiny bottles of antiseptic hand cleanser and passed them out to the family at dinner time.

Sarah mumbled that her uncle had OCD.

"What's that?" asked Braden.

"Something I wish you had," she said.

Rita knew that the thing Rodney had and was trying to protect them against wasn't spread that way, and of course he did too, but she took his excessive cleaning as a gesture of love.

Some nights he didn't come home and often he went out and came in late. Once, after the family had gone to bed, she heard him fumbling in the bathroom, a crash and cursing. She got up before he woke Daryl. She banged on the bathroom door. "You okay?"

"Doing a little housecleaning."

"It's three in the morning."

"I'm alright. Go back to bed, Rita." He sounded sober.

She lay awake in the cold bedroom. Early the next morning she went downstairs and into the bathroom where she cleaned the traces of vomit, the diarrhea that he'd missed. She couldn't help but feel he'd left it for her.

Later he said, "The eighties made an old man of me, Rita. Remember the eighties."

"I had babies then. I wasn't paying attention. You were in New York."

He'd been at Rita and Daryl's two weeks when she carried the boxes from the spare room to the curb for Big Brothers to pick up. He was sullen that morning, though willing to help.

He dropped his box on the sidewalk and caught his breath. "Why do we have so much junk?" He'd taken to rhetorical questions, the "we" no longer meaning he and Rita or the family but all of humanity. He had a bible beside his bed. Rita said nothing.

Because she saw he was out of breath, she sat down on one of the boxes so he would, too. It was warm for March and the street was quiet, mid-morning on a weekday, her neighbours at school and at work.

"You know I never took you for the suburbia type. I always thought you'd be a trapeze artist or walk to the north pole. I wanted a sister like that. Maybe a saint like Theresa or a miracle worker, a magician."

"Sorry to disappoint you."

"No, I'm joking. But come on—Daryl—really, Rita?"

"He's decent, unlike many you've been with. Whatever happened to... ?"

"Don't start on me."

"You started, Rod." She stood up. "I have to get ready for work." Halfway to the front door, she stopped. "Come in. I'll make you lunch before I head off." He sat with his back to her, facing the empty street.

She was frying eggs when he came in the front door and up the stairs to the kitchen.

"Do you mind if I keep this?" he asked. In his hand, he held a wall hanging with the print of a skeleton wearing a sombrero and a brightly coloured blanket. He had sent it to her from Mexico years before: *The Day of the Dead*.

"Oh," she said.

"Not good enough for your posh home?" His knuckles were white where they held the fabric and his cheeks were dark caves.

"I had it for years, don't you remember, hanging in the family room. We painted and we changed the décor."

"You changed the décor."

"It's not like it was worth a lot of money, was it, Rod."

"I should have realized." He spoke in a near whisper.

"Realized what?"

He flung his hands in the air and the wall hanging dropped to the ground. "What you really are."

"I'm just your sister, Rod. I'm sorry about the wall hanging. Let's talk later. I'm going to work."

"Go to work." He stood aside. "While you're gone, I'll sweep your driveway and do your laundry because your spoiled kids do dick."

"You know nothing about kids." She pushed past him where he blocked her in the door. He trembled and his mouth twitched.

"What's the matter with you, Rod? You're being an asshole."

He leapt away from her and down the stairs. Minutes later, he slammed the door and she watched him go down the walk with his bag, shoulders hunched, clothes so loose, his body only hinted at corporality.

"Come back," she couldn't say. Instead, she emailed: *We need a break from one another.* She signed it, *Love, Rita.* She wrote the next day and said, *Come on the trip with us. I'm sorry.* In her haste she forgot to write her name. *Love* was all she wrote.

Shots of sunlight shred the mist. Charlie slows down to veer around a log. The roar of the motor drops and the call of a loon reverberates across the water.

"Where is it?" asks Daryl.

Charlie shrugs, "somewhere out there." He revs the motor and leaves the log bouncing in the skiff's wake.

A blue sea, sharp with shards of sunlight, appears through the dissipating fog. The brightness pains Rita's eyes.

She'd tried to fix things. Emails—no response. She'd heard from Mia that he was staying there. Other than the drinking—"What's with the drinking?"—as far as Mia knew, he was doing all right. "You know he never says much. No, he didn't mention you. I'm staying out of it."

The view across to Vancouver Island is now clear. Charlie accelerates the motor and the skiff slams into the water as if it were not liquid but something impenetrable. Rodney has been dying since he was twenty-six: his death, also his life. Tofino is in sight: a smattering of small buildings straining away from the surrounding forest. Her stomach whirls from the smell of gas and the lurching of the boat.

Why didn't she get that he was dying? When it finally

got said out loud, her friends and Mia would say that there was nothing she could have done. But there was; she could have been kinder. That much she could have done. You can always be kinder.

The boat slows down as they enter the harbour. Daryl jumps out, gravel crunching underfoot, grabs the rope and pulls the skiff ashore. He and Charlie slide the kayaks off the racks. She sees Charlie isn't going to help carry them up to the road. His job is done. She gets out and he passes her a bag. She turns to assist Daryl and he shakes his head, hoists a boat on his shoulder and heads up the ramp.

Charlie sniffles, drags his forearm across his forehead, and looks out to sea. "Good day for a drive."

He takes a twenty from her and pulls away, the boat separating the sea into a frothy crescent. She turns from the water and steps onto the concrete shore.

Crow

"If I don't feel better before Thursday..." said Rodney. And like one of Dali's clocks, his words collapsed into the gray light of the hospital room. Rita glanced away from the slight figure of her brother. His eyes were overlarge in his gaunt face and seemed to hold a question she was sure she couldn't answer. She scanned for her car outside the window in the parking lot. There it was: bright red beneath the overcast sky. She'd lost track of how long she'd been there. She played with the watch that clutched at her wrist. The digital numbers on its face twitched and for a half-second seemed to elongate and collapse. Rita closed her eyes and breathed deeply. When she opened them, the numbers had reconfigured and indicated a new hour. It was time to go.

Thursday Rodney died. One week later before the sun had fully risen, Rita woke to scratching on the gable outside her bedroom window—and the call: that craggy, violent and mocking diatribe.

"Crow," said her husband, Daryl, with his eyes still closed. In his half-awake state, he rubbed her back in the place where it often hurt.

She rolled away from him, climbed out of bed, and went downstairs before her children woke. She stood on the deck and leaned in such a way that she could see the crow, a restless blur in the brightening air. She recalled an image of her mother in a housecoat on the back porch, black hair tumbled around her shoulders holding a piece of burnt toast toward a crow. It had stood on the railing stabbing its beak at her mother's offering. Her mother had called it her pet, and once her father, in a fit of anger, had thrown his coffee at that same crow.

Rita went inside, showered and slipped into a skirt and blouse. She hadn't dressed since after the funeral. When she went downstairs, her son, Braden, sat at the table eating Cheerios.

"You're going back to work?" He was sixteen.

"Yes," she said without looking at him. She ground the coffee beans and spooned some into the coffee maker.

He returned to eating his cereal.

Daryl came down the stairs whistling, the way he did most mornings, his cheerfulness all high decibels and forced breath. At the sight of her, he stopped. "You going to work today?"

"Yes," she said between her teeth.

"Do you think you're ready?" He stood by the coffee maker while it rumbled and spat.

"Why stay home? It's not like anything is going to change."

He shrugged his shoulders and sipped his coffee. "Up to you."

Sarah banged into the kitchen, heavy-footed in a waft of lavender and demands. These days she wanted money for things: jeans, electronic devices, teenage whims. She was the loudest of Rita's two children. Her urgency, as if Rita hadn't noticed it before, was puzzling.

"It's just that you promised me," said Sarah.

"There's been a few things going on around here," said Rita.

Sarah flung back her hair with a sigh. "Mom, you're not listening."

It was as though they were actors in a movie, capable of reverse or fast forward at any moment.

"I have to go," said Rita placing her half-finished coffee on the counter and feeling something like motion sickness.

Rita walked to work across the old bridge over the harbour into downtown. Cyclists in varying fluorescent shades of Lycra and polystyrene darted past her on the pedestrian walkway and on the periphery of her attention—a blur of SUVs and Subarus.

She descended the stairs to the inner harbor where gulls dived and squawked above the masts of small sailboats and American yachts. A young woman erected umbrellas on a patio in front of a restaurant; with a click and a whoosh they bloomed above her. The woman, unconscious of Rita, grabbed a bucket from a metal trolley and began wiping tabletops, striding through her tasks with the same faith in the coming moments and hours of the day that Rita saw in her daughter. Rita imagined Sarah older, the two of them seated at one of the tables on a sunny afternoon, a pitcher of sangria between them, orange slices staining and colliding while ice cubes melted in the blood red wine. A celebration, perhaps. They'd been shopping for something—Sarah loved shopping—something significant like a wedding dress. Rita imagined photographs to hang on her wall until she died. This image pleased Rita even though she'd not bothered with a wedding dress herself. In fact, Rita and Daryl had never bothered with marriage, believing at the time in the moment, or so they told themselves, and from that moment a life had taken shape between them—quick and unbidden.

Rita imagined Sarah appearing from between the curtains in the change room, white satin billowing around her slight body, conviction etched into the line of her jaw, defiance even, as she awaited her mother's praise, and all the time from outside the bridal shop the drone of traffic pressing forward.

She'd been away a week that morning when she entered the classroom at the immigration centre where she taught English. Roshana sat with her eyes closed at the student's table, resting her head on her arms, hair alive with tiny braids. She worked nights as a cleaner and took the early bus in from Colwood, so often napped before class. When Rita dropped her bag on the table at the front of the room, she startled awake.

"Hello, teacher," she said, "you are back, it is good." She stood and walked toward Rita, reached for her, and Rita received her hug, Roshanna's down jacket squishy against her cheek. "I am sad your brother, he die."

"Thank you, Roshana." She stepped back, not knowing what to say to this woman whose family, what was left of them, were missing in Somalia during the worst drought ever, whose oldest brother had died of AIDS, whose youngest brother had died from a gunshot, whose child belonged to a missing sister, whose husband, trained as an X-ray technician, worked nights at Kentucky Fried Chicken. This woman who had never before attended school, who worked nights as a cleaner and came to English language classes all day.

"Still cold, Roshana," said Rita, fingering the woman's jacket. "You've been here for six months now and we haven't even got to winter yet. You're going to have to take the jacket off sometime."

Roshana laughed. "So cold here," she said, shaking her head.

The perfect tenses were the most difficult to teach; *I have lived, I have been living, I will have been living, I haven't lived.* "It's when the past or the future has some relationship to the present," explained Rita. "It's confusing," she said, turning away from her student's puzzled faces.

"So there is really no past and no future," said Muhammed, always the philosopher.

"There is," insisted Rita, tapping her impermanent marker on the white board.

At lunch, Rita sat in the tiny courtyard between the two buildings. One building housed a drop-in centre for people living with HIV and a real estate office. The other housed the immigration centre. The day was warm for September, so Rita removed her jacket and opened her lunch bag. She withdrew a cheese sandwich from the bag and held it in her hand, examining it in the way one examines their face now and then when staring into a mirror. The bread, with its thousand tiny molecules, moved ceaselessly toward decay. How could she eat the sandwich knowing how much it had aged since morning? She sat back with a sigh.

Perhaps, as she usually did, she should have joined the other teachers in the noisy staffroom. But sitting in the courtyard, she didn't feel as alone as she suspected she would if she were in the staffroom. She looked up from her lap and came eye to eye with a crow. She probably wouldn't have noticed as crows are so commonplace, except that the crow she'd seen that morning was fresh in her mind. This crow stood on the concrete not far from her feet. The crow's eyes were so small that they surely couldn't let in that much light. Without light, wondered Rita, what would the crow see. The crow hopped towards her and it was larger than she thought, bolder too. It wanted something from her. She could feel it, something she might not want to give. She followed the crow's line of vision and saw that the crow had its beady eyes on her sandwich.

"No," she said, uneasy about what might happen if she gave in to the crow's demands. It cocked its head this way and that. Could it be the same crow from this morning? It hopped away then stopped in a perfect pose. She thought again of her mother's pet crow. When her father had thrown coffee at it, hadn't he called it a "pansy" for all its preening. Or had he? Now, all these years later, she couldn't be sure. Her brother would have remembered the crow; the two of them had often pieced together fragments of their childhood. In that way he was her memory, and she, his.

The crow before her now stood against a pale wall. Its silhouette made it look like a cut-out from the night as if this daytime world of trees, buildings and people were a cardboard set and if you cut away a shape, any shape you would see this deeper dimension.

One week and one day after her brother died, Rita and Daryl went to Rita's childhood friend, Jill's place for dinner. Jill, and her husband, Jack in a rural suburb just outside of Victoria, where they could be close to nature. Jack and Jill's house met the Leeds green building standard, and this made them comfortable in the assumption that they were stewards of the Earth.

It was the first time Rita had seen Jill since the funeral. Jill pulled Rita against her fulsome bosom and mumbled something about Rodney being in a better place, even though Rita knew Jill never liked him.

With a note of anxiety in her voice, Jill often talked of reductions: garbage and consumer goods, her breasts. True enough, they swung when she walked and gave her a look of timorousness. Like tall people who slouch, she hunched her shoulders as if in an effort to squish them as one does a sleeping bag into a stuff sack. She had too much and she felt bad for it. Her way to deal with it was to drink excessively: red wine, organic, local. Check, check, check...

Rita sunk into their couch and drifted in and out of sleep while around her the conversation turned to the end of the world, as it often did. Jack and Jill belonged to the South Island Sustainable Homeowners or what Daryl called out of earshot of their friends, the SS. Jack had just joined the Sierra Club after reading about a coal mine proposal north of Victoria half way up Vancouver Island. He was a stick of a thing, looked half-starved beside his dumpling-shaped wife. And he was good with statistics.

"If it's approved it will produce 127,500 cubic metres of methane a day," he said.

Jill shook her head and popped another Napolean from the Italian Bakery into her mouth.

Rita couldn't picture 127, 500 cubic metres of methane, though she knew it could not be a good thing.

"Hmm... Have you seen the iPhone fours yet?" said Daryl. "Stunning graphics."

"Don't they make steel from coal," said Rita. "Didn't you know that, Daryl," she said, sliding her leg across the cushions and toeing the flesh on his thigh. Daryl glanced at her, his lips quivering in a half-grin.

Jill sipped her wine with a gulp.

"Of the 222 projects that the environmental-assessment office has handled since 1995, only one was rejected," said Jack, his gaze on the ceiling, as if addressing God.

In the kitchen, Jill told Rita about an organic gardening club she had joined and expressed her concerns about the diminishing supply of food on the planet. "At no other time in history... " she said and something else, but Rita had trouble paying attention.

"There will be no future," said Jill, her fat hands plunging into the sudsy water.

The function of the modal verb *will* is prediction, thought Rita, lowering a heavy pot into a drawer. Or it can mean fortitude. With a soft whoosh, the door slid back into the cabinet.

As Daryl and Rita pulled out of the driveway, Jack and Jill waved from their front room window.

"Good-night Saint Jack, the world will sleep easier tonight knowing you are in it," said Daryl, waving.

Rita peered through the passenger's side window into blackness. "You should care," she said.

"About what?"

"About the world, about the future. Like they do."

"I care about my family, don't I? I recycle. What is this, Rita? Jack's a smug tight ass who cares more about his ego than he does the world. We've always agreed on that."

"Why do we even go there, listen to them, eat their food, make fun of them afterwards?" The trees that lined the narrow road loomed black and physical. She longed to be amongst headlights, traffic lights, lighted windows.

"She's your old friend, remember."

"She's an airhead." She winced at her own cruelty.

"It's a good thing she is, or she'd realize what an idiot he is."

"Why do we go?"

"It's just what we do."

In the dashboard light with all the darkness of the country road pressing on the car windows, Daryl's face blurred into shadows making him appear a stranger.

"Rita," he said, "you cared."

His voice took her by surprise. "What?"

"You cared enough. It was enough. For your brother."

She pressed her nose hard against the cold window. They burst onto the highway and shafts of light from the traffic sliced through the car's interior.

A week and a half after her brother's death, on a Monday

morning, Rita asked her class, "What do you do on the weekends?"

"We go to sister-in-law birthday party," said Baljeet, all smiles.

"No," said Rita, remembering to smile back. What do you *usually* do on the weekend?"

"Different," said Baljeet, nodding.

"I clean the house. I go to Thrifty's, buy groceries, I make wash clothes, I go to swimming with my little girl and Sunday I go to church," said Roshana. "Same all the time." She threw up her hands and rolled her eyes.

"Over and over and over," said Rita, also rolling her eyes and the class laughed. "We use the simple present to talk about routines." They knew this but students slipped so easily into the wrong tenses. She demonstrated on the board, her own weekends there, capsulated and ordered in an impossible way.

On Saturdays, I get up at 9:00. I take my son to soccer practice at 10:00. In the afternoon, I go grocery shopping. At night we rent a movie and order pizza. On Sundays we sleep in. She stood staring at her words on the board as if puzzled by whose life the words might represent.

"Sometimes different," said Muhammed.

"Of course," she said, turning to the class with a smile, "and if something happens out of the ordinary, like a birthday party for example, what tense do we use?"

"Now it is past," said Muhammed.

She nodded, and she could see that he enjoyed saying *now* and *past* in the same sentence.

My brother dies, my brother died, now my brother has died. She didn't write it on the board.

Roshana stayed behind after class. "Teacher Rita," she said, "my sister and mother go to Kenya. I hear from my uncle in Nairobi."

"Are they okay, Roshana?"

"They alive, Teacher," said Roshana, placing her hand on Rita's arm as if comforting her.

Rita skipped the staff meeting and drove instead to Mt. Doug where she walked on the beach. Close to shore a kayak needled its way through a low mist; its orange fiberglass flanks, the top half of its occupant and the paddle's slow rotation appeared to be parts of a single creature, alien to its watery surroundings.

She crossed the road to the forest trails and took the path leading to the summit.

She strode upwards as if she were walking, not toward, but, against something. By the first switchback, she doubled over with the fire in her lungs, and the sweat that slimed her face and pooled beneath her arms. She slid on a rock, righted herself, and carried on, biting her bottom lip until it stung, seizing her breath from the forest air. She pounded hard on the path wanting to feel the bones pressing the inside of her skin: pain moving from inside out and shedding like sweat, like water running off a surface.

Finally, near the top of the mountain she gave out on a moss-covered outcropping. On her back, she felt her heart beat hard in her chest and her scraped lungs and muscles give way. She drifted into half-sleep and woke to a chain of unbroken cawing. A crow on a nearby rock jerked its head in her direction. She sat up just as it lifted and flew to the branches of a fir where some fifty or sixty crows had gathered at various heights, with more arriving. They fluttered their wings spilling a deep shade from the high reaches of the tree. In the way we search for someone in a crowd, she tried to distinguish between them, to delineate large from small, loud from soft, to notice the difference in their calls. Was there something she could recognize, a familiar cock of the head, the flutter of a wing, a way of taking flight? She realized, as crazy as it seemed, that she was looking for *the* crow. If there were differences, to Rita's eye they were minute: this one slightly fluffier, that one shinier and that one calmer.

After awhile, as if they had accepted her presence, the crow's cacophony dwindled to a muddled constant. A murder, a murder of crows is what it's called. She sat for several minutes before getting to her feet. The path meandered for a ways along the summit then descended into the thickness of the forest. The closer she came to the parking lot, the less distinctive the bird sounds were and more ordinary. Soon she could hear only traffic. At the bottom of the mountain, several people in what appeared to be a running group, were gathered. She found her car amongst the many that were now in the parking lot where she'd left it beneath a shedding arbutus. As she climbed in, she felt lighter as if she herself had shed an old skin and left it on the mountain: an offering to the crows.

She pulled into rush hour traffic and pushed the radio button as a voice announced the top-of-the-hour newscast. Not much had changed in the world in the two weeks since she'd last listened. She cast her thoughts back over her workday then forward to plan dinner. This coming weekend, she would take Sarah shopping for jeans.

On the dashboard clock the numbers jittered forward. There would be no stopping them.

Erosion

Marie sits on her deck at the cabin and thinks about erosion. When Brice, her husband, arrives, she'll show him how the stacks of shale that form the bank are crumbling. He'll see how the bank sags away from the sea, as if recoiling from a force far greater than itself.

Though the sky is darkening she can't go in. Earlier, the sudden showers, the clouds crowding and bumping into one another, the restless water from the wind's persistent wrangling kept her in the cabin: tidying, trying to read, drinking one coffee after the other. Now the surface of the sea has resolved into a skin of silk. As if they've absorbed the day's agitations, the rocks on the shore are volcanic black. The clouds, piled high on the horizon, are still and remote as an inukshuk. Even the birds are silent in this silver light. She and the sea have paused.

At the first roll of thunder she startles and glances at her watch. It's almost seven. Brice will arrive soon with Mel, whom, she recalls with some weariness, has had another break-up. This means that she will get her daughter to herself, no boyfriend, this time, but Mel is twenty-two and has not yet learned to rise and fall with life's vicissitudes. Do we ever? Mel will expect something of her mother, some rendering of her bleak mood, an acknowledgement of worth and blame, something of which Marie is certain she'll fall short.

She's counting on Brice to put Mel in a good mood on their way up the island. He's a good father. He's not interested in Mel's personal life, but he makes her laugh as he used to make Marie laugh. Some days Marie is jealous and then she's ashamed for feeling jealous of her own daughter. She talks to Brice on Wednesday evenings from the payphone at the gas station up on the highway.

"Oh, hi," he says, as if he's forgotten she was going to phone.

"How's work?" she says.

Usually he says "fine." Sometimes he tells her about a small problem, though she doesn't listen because he works with seismographs and other instruments to measure vibrations within the Earth and she finds it all too technical. When they were engaged, Marie derived some comfort from knowing that her future husband would be able to warn her and the family about the *big one*, the earthquake that was most certainly going to occur in the Pacific Northwest sometime within the next five hundred years. Every now and then at the school where she teaches, they have an earthquake drill and all the children have to "duck, cover, and hold," which means crawling under their desks to avoid falling debris.

She's come to think of her summer alone at the cabin as her own version of duck, cover, and hold.

This past Wednesday, Brice had remembered to ask her how she was feeling.

"Do you mind me being up here?" was her answer.

"No, no, I understand." He's often relieved when she deflects from the feeling question. She doesn't know why she does it because she tells him that she wants him to ask.

"What do you understand?" The windows of the phone booth were smeared with a paste of dust and grime, so she couldn't see out. On the glass near the phone were fingered the words; *If you're not living on the edge, you're taking up too much space.* It would have taken someone a lot of persistence to trace the tiny words into the grime with the tip of their finger just as it would also take a lot of persistence to live by such a maxim.

Brice and Mel want her to carry a cellphone, but she insists she doesn't need one.

"Well... " said Brice. They'd agreed that she was depressed, though he hadn't been able to say the word until she'd come home and told him that the doctor had prescribed Celexa, an anti-depressant. Somehow this made it so. Brice had no experience dealing with depressed people, and Marie, as far as she knew, had no experience being depressed, at least not in the way that the feeling was no longer something that you had, but something that you became. *I am depressed,* she'd whispered in the mirror to herself when she got home.

It had been a five-minute appointment with the doctor.

"I can't sleep."

"Hmm."

"I've got no energy."

"Anything else?" said Dr. Smyth, writing on a chart.

"I cry a lot."

Dr. Smyth looked up. She was younger than Marie with her hair tied back and glasses half way down her nose. She never smiled. "Any history of depression?"

"No."

"Thoughts of suicide."

"No. A feeling of lethargy, of being bored out of my mind," said Marie. "Tired of waiting... waiting... for something to happen." She cried right there in the doctor's office.

The young doctor stared at her for a moment and then wrote a prescription for Celexa. Marie walked out of the office clutching the prescription in one hand and with the other blowing her nose on a Kleenex the doctor had given her—embarrassed. Who goes on antidepressants for boredom?

The fact was she'd only taken the pills for a few days and had such terrible heart palpitations and such a debilitating fear that some disaster was about to occur that she'd stopped. She hadn't told her doctor because she'd been warned that initially there might be some side effects that would shortly go away and she knew Dr. Smyth would encourage her to wait it out. But if there were going to be any waiting it out, Marie would rather wait out whatever was causing the disruption on her emotional barometer. After all, much of life was waiting, wasn't it? She'd waited to get married, to have children, to get a permanent position with the school district, to get a raise, to buy the house and for Mel to start school, finish school, start university, for Brice to get a promotion, to buy the cabin. And there were all the little waits: waiting for Friday, the mail to come, for coffee break, an evening out with a girlfriend, for time alone with her husband, a returned phonecall or email, time alone with her daughter, for summer, for sex, Christmas, her birthday, the two weeks at the cabin, for her anger to abate.

Sometimes she wonders if Brice actually believes that being able to measure the size of an earthquake and make a relative prediction will mitigate the impact, the devastation. Depression and Celexa: that's what she offered him, packaged, like a gift.

"Well," he'd said again on the end of the telephone line. She heard the tap water and pictured the kitchen sink in her Gordon Head home. "You need to get away, to get some perspective. It's fine, don't worry, it's fine."

It's where they end up and stay, always with, "it's fine." She imagined him looking at his watch, out the front room window then leafing through the paper.

"I'll be up Friday," he said, his voice softer.

She knows he feels responsible and it's not really him. Whenever her girlfriends complain about their husbands, she feels lucky that hers isn't like that. And yet it is him because it's been him for twenty-seven years now.

The sky rumbles up and down the inlet. A few minutes later a sheet of lightning trembles above the mountains on the mainland. She loves the drama of a thunderstorm. Sometimes she even imagines the deep shaking of a quake and the sea gathering into a massive wave coming towards her up the inlet. Brice tells her that there are 1200 earthquakes a year recorded in BC, earthquakes too small for most people's awareness. There won't be a big one in her lifetime.

Finally the rain lets loose from the clouds and pounds into the dry earth. She hears the car in the drive. Pulling a rain jacket over her head she runs to the front of the cabin to meet her family.

"Oh—my—god—I thought we were going to get hit by lightening," says Mel, her long legs swinging out of the passenger's side. "Hey, Mom." She flings her arms outward, one landing on Marie's shoulder, the other around her waist. Her daughter is at least an inch taller than her now. Marie returns the hug, attempting to pull the girl in tight. But Mel is impatient and Marie sees she's invigorated by the storm.

"Hurry," says Marie, "or you'll get soaked." Brice pecks Marie on the cheek and grabs bags from the trunk.

Marie pours three glasses of wine and herds daughter and husband out onto the covered deck where just beyond, the rain is a steady downpour. Brice lights a coal oil lamp and smiles down at her. He's a tall man and though his hair is receding and he seems to get thinner and more gangly each year, his eyes remain startling, subterranean. It's what first drew him to her. Once, when they were classmates, just before Brice had asked her out, Marie, sitting with her girlfriends at the student pub, had told them that there was something sexy about a man who understands the movements of the tectonic plates deep in the core of the Earth. She'd purred the word *Earth*, and thrust her breasts forward. She was a cute blonde then.

They talk about Mel's summer job as a camp counsellor; what courses she wants to take next year. She likes the sciences but also wants to be a teacher like her mother.

"There's nothing wrong with teaching. It's an honorable career," says Brice. The lantern sputters.

Later, after Brice has drifted off and Marie thinks Mel has, too, her daughter's voice surprises her.

"What do you do up here, Mom?

"I read. I walk. I've been cleaning up a corner of the yard for a garden. I'm keeping a journal."

"Hmmm." Mel's eyes drift toward the sea, dark now, and quiet except for the sibilance of the lessening rain. "I'd be bored to tears. When are you coming home?"

"How are you feeling about the break-up?" says Marie, pulling her sweater around her.

"I don't want to talk about it." She'd been dating Paul, a boy she knew from high school, for three years. They'd broken up many times.

Marie is silent, trying to think of what she's supposed to say and really wanting to go to bed.

Mel slumps in her chair with a loud sigh. "Paul's never going to do anything with his life except work at Thrifty Foods."

"No." Marie is cautious.

"This time is for good, Mom. I know it was the right thing, but it doesn't mean it doesn't hurt."

Marie reaches her hand towards her daughter's hand. Mel pulls away.

"Dad says you're on antidepressants and I shouldn't bother you with things. Do I bother you with things? What do you have to be depressed about?" Mel stares at her mother, eyes flashing—her father's eyes. She's sitting forward in her chair.

"No, no, of course you don't. I'm your mother."

"What does that mean?"

What does it mean? "That I love you and want to listen to you." Her voice is pinched and she is afraid she's spoken it like a question.

"So what happened? It's not like anybody died or you lost your job or anything."

Marie wrings her hands. "I know it's hard to understand. I'll be fine." Both women stare into the dark. The bushes rustle—a raccoon, likely—but they can't see in the dark.

After about five minutes, Mel clicks her tongue and gets to her feet. "I'm off to bed."

With a loud snore, Brice jerks his head. Marie tidies up glasses. A rough-throated heron rasps on the shore.

Brice wants to go to Santorini. He's spread brochures about Greece out on the table in the small cabin. The wind and rain slash against the window. He'd been thinking about it, she sees now, probably since her doctor's appointment. They haven't been anywhere for years, had come to the cabin every summer for two or three weeks and on weekends.

"Isn't it an earthquake zone?" Outside the waves leap toward the bank. Oh, she must talk to him about the bank. He was asleep by the time she got to bed last night. He's always so tired on Fridays. She pours the two of them coffee.

"Always small ones, but there hasn't been a bad one since 1956." He's looking for a photograph. He likes to show her pictures of devastation from earthquakes.

"Today, Santorini is the only inhabited caldera in the world. Do you know what that is?"

Marie watches the storm outside the window. "Caldera...
cauldron," she says.

"A collapse after a volcanic eruption, like a crater. Villages
on the island line the edge of the caldera." He steps to her
side and shows her a photo from the brochure, not of
devastation, but of a couple toasting glasses of wine above an
Aegean blue sea, surrounded by sparkling white buildings
atop a high cliff.

"Hmm," she says and glances up at him.

He's watching for her reaction. "You live in an earthquake
zone," he says.

"I know." She touches his face. The bristles on his cheek
are sharp. She moves away to clear the table.

Brice has built up the fire in the wood stove. The small cabin
is close and hot, smells of smoke. Marie can't concentrate
on the Monopoly game. The cheeriness between father and
daughter is false, put on for her sake. The more they try the
more she resists.

"Mom, Dad's cheating, I know he is! Watch him count
his money." Mel's voice is high-pitched, hysterical.

The wind shakes the window at the kitchen table where
they sit. The glass is white with condensation. Marie sighs
and wipes away a little square. The line of cedars and firs
lean away from the bank. Out on the sea the waves toss and
wrestle with one another. "Is this ever going to stop?" she
says, getting up to plug in the kettle again.

"Relax, come play," says Brice. He pats the chair beside
him.

There was a time when Marie was happy as long as her
family was happy. That's all it took. "I'm going outside," she
says.

Brice and Mel look up from their game.

"Mom, it's miserable out, and you've got Park Place and Board Walk. You could break us."

"I'm not landing there," says Brice, crossing his arms and bugging his eyes at his daughter.

"Everybody does sooner or later, Dad," Mel says, shaking her finger at her father.

"Honey, I'll go down to the beach with you when we're finished the game." Marie hears the impatience in his voice. She isn't playing by the rules.

"You guys go ahead. I need some air." She throws on her raincoat and boots. "Don't forget about the kettle."

She's out the door before they can say anything else and on the stairs that lead down to the beach. She gasps at the force of the wind and rain and her foot slides on the saturated wooden stairs. On the beach she picks her way over the slippery rocks toward the breaking surf. Usually the surf is insignificant as the inlet is protected by two small islands that take the brunt of its battering from the open sea, but not today. Today the breakers curl around the guardian islands and tumble in her direction. She tries to imagine the distance and the tonnage of water, the silent unseen mountains and troughs far down in the depths of the ocean between her and Japan, 7000 kilometres away. At the water line the clamorous exchange between wind and sea fills her ears. The waves hurl themselves at the shore.

She sees, in her mind's eye, her body rising above the waves, now a kite at the whim of the wind's pull and drag. It's what she wants, but her feet are heavy on the shore and out of her comes a low, loud wail. She screams again then again and the sound carries across the sea.

A low rumble followed by the babel of descending soil and stone comes from behind. She turns to see a fir tree plunge off the bank, its bulging root dragging stacks of shale and earth. It bounces once and rests on the shore. Behind it, the bank gives way. Mounds of earth and shale collapse in a heap near the fallen tree and on the bottom steps leading up from the beach. With the wind at her back she runs towards the stairs.

Brice appears on the top of the bank. He steps quickly down the stairs, slips and lands on the mound of earth at the bottom. She runs faster now. He's on his feet again and shouting but she can't hear what he's saying. He gestures for her to go back. He struggles over the mound of dirt and glances behind him at the gouge in the bank. As he gets closer she sees his face is streaked with mud and his t-shirt is plastered against his skin. He's wearing only sandals and has not taken the time to put on his coat. She stops and watches him struggle toward her. She's not been able to keep the hood of her jacket on her head and wet, heavy strands of hair whip her face. When he reaches her he grips her elbow and digs his thumb into her arm. She winces and tries to pull away. His skin smells cold.

"Holy shit," shouts Mel who is not far behind her dad, laughing and dipping her outstretched arms as if they're wings. "Mom and Dad, I'm leaving for Mozambique in September. Thought I should tell you." She spins and shrieks in the wind.

"What?" asks Marie, and she can't help smiling.

"I've got a teaching job. ESL."

"Mozambique's a dangerous country," says Brice. "Landmines." He lets go of Marie.

"The war's been over for years, Dad."

Brice is shivering. "Let's go back and talk about this."

Mel's cheeks are flushed and her eyes are shining. She bounces backwards, turns and runs toward the house shouting over her shoulder, "Nothing to talk about, Dad." Marie laughs and sprints after her daughter.

The next day dawns clear with a sea that is smooth and spent. Mel recovers pieces of shale from the pile on the beach and builds an inukshuk on the edge of the bank where it's been carved away. Marie plucks a stone from the shore and places it on top, expecting it to tumble. Brice holds several in his hand, comparing their weights and shapes before adding his. When he does, the structure wobbles.

Speaking Underwater

Roan's mother has been gone two mornings now. He knows because the day she didn't come home and the day he discovered the seal were the same day and that was two days ago. If she'd been home and out of bed, she might not have let him come down here.

"It's not safe, Roe," she'd have said, "You're only ten."

Sometimes she gets up with him and sometimes she's already up because she's been up all night. She sits at the kitchen table, smoking, wearing Denny's big red t-shirt that has "*Normal's not Normal*" written on the front and she stinks like a grown-up in the morning. She stares off into space and Roan could do anything and she wouldn't notice.

He's sitting on a log below the ridge of blackberry bushes and the seal is maybe a metre away. He doesn't want to get too close because he's afraid it's dead and he's never seen anything dead, at least anything bigger than an insect. And he's always been the kind of kid who doesn't like to kill spiders. He wishes he wasn't like that.

If you didn't know it was there you'd think the seal was a bulging black rock behind a log, except this morning it smells worse than ever, worse than the beach always smells, like rotting fish. Yesterday the seal turned his head slowly and looked at him and made a funny kind of moaning noise. It startled Roan, but he couldn't look away.

Once his mom told him that you should just leave a beached seal alone, that it'll find it's way back into the water. If it's a baby like this one—it's not very big—it might be waiting for its mom. Today the seal is quiet and doesn't look at him, but he thinks he sees its body moving up and down as if it's still breathing.

On really quiet mornings like this you can hear the clams spitting and the little crabs scurrying under the rocks, the sand falling off their backs and the ocean that's always moving even when it's still. Roan scans the surface of the sea for a sign of the seal pup's mom, but he only sees the water tremor a little with the changing tide.

Roan is supposed to phone his grandma when his mother doesn't come home, but she'll make him go to her house. His grandma doesn't like him going there anymore than he likes going there. She tells him about her bad heart all the time or she mumbles mean things about his mom and phones the police. "I've had enough, Roan," she says, and he's not sure if she means of him or his mother or of something that has nothing to do with them. When his mom finally gets back she and Grandma have a screaming match. Once his grandma said that his mother's going to end up dead in a ditch. In the last couple of days Roan has checked the ditches on his way down to the beach. He's afraid of ditches because there's so little you can see in a ditch and yet you know that whole lives are lived under the long grass, under the smelly stream of water.

He's glad that the seal is above the tide line. It must have been washed up in a storm but Roan doesn't know how long it's been there. It's October and there was frost on the ground this morning. But there's no wind and the tide is barely coming up the beach so the seal's going nowhere. He wants the seal to go back to the ocean but he also wants it to wait until his mother comes back so he can show her.

The secretary at the school phoned yesterday, but Roan hung up as soon as he heard her voice. He hates school. Nobody ever talks to him and he doesn't talk to anybody. People talk too much. Especially Denny, his mom's boyfriend, and he tries to get Roan to talk.

"Hey little buddy, how's it hanging?" He doesn't know what Denny means by that, but he thinks he's talking about Roan's penis. What an idiot. "Your mom's not feeling good today, so why don't you and me get a Starbucks." Roan likes the caramel Frappuchinos. They leave his mom in bed and go to the Starbucks near the beach. Denny always gets a Mocha. Sometimes Roan has to pay because Denny doesn't have enough money. Roan uses the money he gets from his grandma for his birthday and hides it so Denny or his mom can't find it.

Denny is skinny like his mom and his muscles twitch and jerk. He smokes all the time so they have to sit outside at Starbucks on the patio even when it's raining. Sometimes Denny calls his mom a *cunt*. "She doesn't know how lucky she is having me." One time he told Roan that his mother was the best lay he'd ever had. When he's not talking about his mother he's telling Roan how he's going to get on *American Idol*. Denny loves *American Idol* and he loves *Grand Theft Auto*. Roan plays with him when his mom isn't paying attention cause she read somewhere that it's not good for him and she makes him stop by screaming at Denny not to bring his fucking violent games into her house. Roan's not the only one who thinks Denny's an idiot. His mom calls Denny a "fucking airhead" and throws his clothes out of the apartment. When Denny's gone she cleans up the house and goes to twelve-step meetings. She makes Roan clean his room and go to school, then takes him down to the wharf where they buy fish heads for fifty cents from the fisherman and throw them at the seals. The seals at the wharf are not afraid of people because they know they're going to be fed. They swim close to the edge of the wharf, make grunting noises and open their mouths. His mom says the only time Roan looks happy is when he's feeding the seals. She says he must have been a seal in his past life. He likes the idea of living in the ocean and being able to disappear deep into the water and then only appear once in awhile.

Roan and the seal are at one end of a long gravelly beach, where it's quiet and you can't walk anymore. The tide comes right up to the bank, which is covered in blackberries that nobody can reach so they rot on the vine before the summer is over. Roan's grandma lives in what Denny calls a "fancy home" at the other end of the beach. His grandma says it's Cape Cod style. His mom grew up there, but she says the house is stupid because it tries to be something that it's not. The only thing Roan likes about it is the hammock on the veranda.

He and his mom live in a one-bedroom basement suite five blocks from his grandma's house. Roan gets the bedroom and his mom sleeps on the couch in the living room. A bunch of students from the university live upstairs. They have a lot of parties, and one time his mom tried to get herself invited. He was asleep in his room, and this guy came into the apartment with Roan's mom leaning on him and talking non-stop. The guy poked his head into the bedroom. "Hey, Buddy, you alright?" he said. "Looks like your mom needs to sleep it off."

A woman, as old as his grandma, steps off the stairs onto the beach. A tiny dog on a leash strains towards Roan and starts yapping, and the old woman tries to shush him. Roan wants them to go away. He doesn't know what the little dog might do to the seal. He's going to show his mom the seal when she comes home. If the old woman phones the people who take seals away and he ever sees her again he'll throw a rock at her.

The next day his grandmother comes and takes him to her house. He sleeps in his mother's old room. He tries to imagine his mother there but he can't. There's nothing in it that Roan associates with his mother. There's no crossword books or cigarettes, colorful toques—his mother even wears toques in the summer because she's always cold—no pictures of him, not like in their apartment where the fridge is covered with pictures of Roan. His mother's grade twelve diploma is in a frame on the wall. Beside it is a diploma for academic achievement. Roan has never got an academic achievement award.

In the morning his grandmother makes pancakes. She doesn't make him go to school and she lets him watch whatever show he wants on TV. He's watching a rerun of *Family Guy* when his grandmother tells him to come into the kitchen. A woman with dark, grey-streaked hair pulled back into a ponytail is sitting at the table. She smiles at him and says hello. His grandma tells him that the woman is a social worker. She has one eye that doesn't move and Roan doesn't know which eye to look at while she talks to him, so he looks at his hands in his lap. He wishes she wouldn't lean toward him that way. It makes him think he should look at her and he doesn't want to. He settles on looking over her shoulder at the kitchen counter cluttered with his grandmother's things: bottles of pills from the pharmacy, the toaster and coffeemaker, her puffy black purse from which he steals Tic Tacs. He wants to look at his grandmother on the other side of the kitchen table, but then she would know that he wasn't listening, and she told him that it's important that he listens. The woman's words sound like how he imagines a voice would sound under water. Once he tried speaking underwater but he only came up choking with his throat feeling raw.

At the foster home he sits in his closet and imagines that he's the seal on the beach and his mother comes and takes him back to the water. The social worker comes to visit him once a week.

"Your mother's in a treatment centre," she says. She's brought him a new pair of boots. They're green with yellow rim around the tops and yellow-coloured soles.

"Do you know what that is?" She means the treatment centre and not the boots. She's leaning too close to him again, but he thinks that she's trying to be kind.

"Can I go visit her?" He slides one boot over each hand and catches them on the inside of his elbows so that they are like puppets, their toes facing the social worker.

"Not just yet, Roan. She needs to settle in. But soon."

"Can I visit the seal?"

The social worker wrinkles the skin above her nose between her eyes. "What seal?"

"The one at the end of the beach."

"What beach?"

What an airhead. Roan sighs and flings the boots onto the floor and the toe of one of them nicks the social worker's leg. She winces and clears her throat.

"Bobby can take you to the beach." Bobby is the foster father. He's fat and talks too much. Roan stares at the social worker's dead eye.

She shifts in her seat. "How are you feeling about all this, Roan?"

"Will you take me to the beach?" She doesn't get it, this woman, but he likes her better than Bobby.

She slides on her coat. "I'll talk to Bobby," she says, and does up the buttons. "You can talk to Bobby and Diane, Roan. You can tell them how you feel."

Diane always talks about feeling tired. She has two other foster children older than Roan and two of her own children who are too little for Roan to be interested in playing with.

He has been at Diane and Bobby's for two weeks and he's afraid the seal will be dead or gone back out to sea. He finds Bobby in the garage.

"What do they do with dead seals on the beach?" Roan asks Bobby.

"I don't know," he says. "I guess they take them out in the ocean and throw them overboard."

"I'm going to be cremated and thrown overboard," says Roan.

"You're kind of young to be thinking about that." Bobby is leaning over the engine of one of his cars. He has three old cars and he's always telling Roan about them even though it's boring. He stands back from the car and drops the hood. It falls with a bang. A wrench dangles from his hand.

"There's a seal washed up on the beach," says Roan.

"It happens," says Bobby, placing the wrench in the long red toolbox. "Maybe it's sick or injured."

"Maybe it got hit by a boat," says Roan.

"Maybe. When did you see it?"

"Two weeks ago. Can we go to the beach?"

"What beach?"

"Near my old house."

"It'll be dead Roan, or gone. "

"I want to go see."

Bobby puts his hands on his hips and sighs. "How about on the weekend? We can go get ice cream."

"I don't want ice cream. It'll be gone by then."

"It's probably gone already, Roan. If the birds and the maggots haven't taken care of it, Fisheries would've removed it."

Roan stares at him hard.

Bobby looks away and shrugs. "Maybe it's gone back

out to sea." He smiles and brushes his hand through Roan's
hair.

Roan doesn't like Bobby. He's an idiot.

At the treatment centre, he and his mom sit in the cafeteria
and the lady from the kitchen brings him a piece of chocolate
cake. She calls him, *Dear*. His mom is wearing a purple cotton
toque and a big sweatshirt. She's shaking more than usual.
The necklace he bought her at Christmas hangs around her
neck. It has a tiny gold angel on a chain. He bought it with
money from his Grandma at the card shop in the mall. His
mom watches him eat. She takes the hand that isn't holding
the fork and holds it tight.

"I haven't been a very good mom, hey, Roe."

He puts a forkful of cake in his mouth. The cake is sweet
and the icing creamy. On the other side of the cafeteria, the
social worker pours herself a coffee. He doesn't want to look
at his mom. When he finally looks up she is staring at him
and her eyes are watery. Her nose is running, she has sores
around her mouth, and thick dark lines beneath her eyes.

At the door to the treatment centre he puts his arms
around her and squeezes. His head is right under her chin.
She laughs at the grip he has around her waist, and says,
"Easy, Roan." He can feel her bones and he knows now he's
big enough to hurt her.

On Sunday his grandmother comes for him. "Just for
dinner," she reminds him twice in the car on the way to
her house on the beach. "And no going on about that seal.
You know your grandmother's heart is too bad for her to go
traipsing down the beach."

The rain streaks the car windows and outside the trees
sway back and forth. He's wearing his new boots.

"I'll go myself," he says.

"No, you won't, Roan. Those days are over. Now, if you had a friend with you—maybe. You're too much of a loner. Things are going to get better. Diane and Bobby, they seem like nice people. You're lucky."

Roan doesn't feel lucky. He wants to move back into the basement suite with his mother.

While his grandmother is busy making dinner and Roan is supposed to be watching TV, he pulls on his boots and raincoat. Outside the basement door the wind slaps his face. The surf scurries up the beach tossing mounds of rank smelling seaweed on the shore. The tide is high and Roan has to hug the bank and skirt along the piles of driftwood, and it's already dark. When he gets there he's going to move the seal himself. He'll move it up the bank where it's hidden, so he can show his mom when she comes home. He can use a piece of driftwood like a lever, the way the teacher showed them at school.

It only takes him about fifteen minutes to get to the spot where he thought the seal should be. But in the dark it looks different and he's never seen the tide so high. The waves are pushing logs into one another. There's no beach for him to walk on, and behind on the bank only a wall of blackberry bushes. The seal has to be somewhere near. The storm didn't take it. No, there'd been other storms. It had only been a couple of weeks. It wouldn't be decayed yet. But there's no seal in sight. The sea sweeps the gravel clean when it sucks back the surf. Water roils around his feet and pours into the tops of his boots. He scrambles onto the logs, the tears coming fast now. The log jerks in the surf and he falls landing on a fleshy mound that stinks like dead fish. His hands graze the slimy back of what he knows to be the seal. Roan screams and jumps to his feet. Squinting, he tries to make out the shape in the dark, touches the body again, waiting for the in and out of breath but there's nothing.

He finds a long flat piece of driftwood, shoves the end of it beneath the body of the seal and pushes until he feels its bulk roll against the wood then continues pushing, his face soaked with tears, sweat and rain. Finally, the surf grabs the seal and Roan can no longer feel its weight.

Roan couldn't have found a safe spot on land. The ocean is too high, too powerful. It's better that the seal moves toward the ocean's quiet depths, better than rotting here on land. His mother will never see the seal.

He stops crying.

The Promise of Water

An accident on the Malahat sends me on a detour around Shawnigan Lake, and I discover that my uncle's house is still standing: as much a shamble as it was thirty years ago. And not five minutes down the road, I recognize the Legion—a brutish building without windows that sits on a patch of cracked asphalt.

When you come west, you go back in time. It's almost noon in Toronto where I got on the plane last night, and here the shops in the village clustered at one end of the lake are just opening. I can't sleep when I travel, and I've still got an hour's drive to Mom's house, so I pull into a coffee shop. Faded posters on the door flap in the breeze advertising a Reiki practitioner, a farmer's market and bands that played two months ago, in the summer. The tourists have all gone home.

I get a coffee from the sleepy, gray-haired woman behind the counter.

"Cold this morning," she says.

"Not when you come from Toronto."

"Snow there?"

"Not yet, but it's coming."

I take my coffee outside and on my way to the stairs that lead to the dock, I stop where a small grocery store once stood above the wharf. Aunt Mary used to take my cousins,

Ted and Danny, and me there after swimming all day. She'd buy cigarettes for herself and fudgicles, rashed with frost, for us boys. Our fingers and toes were wrinkled from hours in the water, our bathing suits still damp against our skin. Ted, the oldest, was a fish like his mom, and he always said he was going to join a swim team—that he'd one day swim in the Olympics.

"Soon as I save up enough money, Ted's taking lessons," Mary said to me more than once.

She worked at the Lakeshore nursing home three nights a week. Her paycheques held them over when the woods were closed for fire season and Uncle Roy was laid off.

Today the air is cool, the lake restless and reedy smelling. My thoughts drift to my mother, her bad hip, the year since Dad died, how lonely she sounds on the phone. Maybe I should move back. I haven't told her about the break-up with Joyce and how Tammi, Mom's only grandchild, won't speak to me, her own father. I don't know how things got so bad between Joyce and I. One day your life is just your life, for better or for worse, and the next it's blown to bits. How does that happen? Joyce said I never saw it coming because I never paid attention. I guess Tammi agrees with her: fifteen and thinks she's got everything figured out. The water undulates in rainbows of gasoline – too many boats now. I settle into a wobbly Adirondack chair and sip my coffee. I feel as worn as the grey boards beneath my feet. The wharf shifts under a gust of wind.

It occurs to me that I, like Tammi, was fifteen the last time I was here. It was the summer my parents went to Las Vegas for a week. Dad drove me from Nanaimo to my Uncle's house, Elvis blasting on an eight-track, and I remember I wouldn't speak to him the entire drive because I could think of about one hundred and one better ways to spend a week in the summer than with my younger cousins. When Mom wasn't around,

Dad called my aunt and uncle hillbillies and made jokes about Uncle Roy having a still in the woods. He said Aunt Mary, my mom's sister, was ok, and I should be good to her and help with the boys, for my mom's sake. Mom worried a lot about her younger sister and said those boys were wild and I was a good influence. When we got to my aunt and uncle's place, Dad, impatient for his holiday, dumped me in the dusty driveway, sped off in a cloud of dust, and left me face to face with Uncle Roy.

"Nice car your dad's got." Roy had a way of tilting his forehead when he spoke that forced his eyeballs up to the tops of their sockets. He stunk of Brylcream and Lucky Lager beer, hunched his shoulders like a man who couldn't live up to his long limbs. "Fancy government job. Guess he can afford it."

At that moment, Mary stepped out of the house, exhaling, "Honey" and "Sweetie" like dandelion seed and kissed my cheeks, my lips. She kissed everyone that way. She must have only been in her late twenties or early thirties then, at least ten years younger than Roy. I stood a whole head and shoulders above her, and she made a big deal about my height, my curly hair. "Oh, you heartbreaker you," she said. "You must have a hundred girlfriends." She looked like she was holding back laughter, her full and painted lips quivering. It made me feel a fool, though now I see that finding her way to the comical was Mary's faith, what helped her to live with Roy.

Mary took me into the house where I dumped my bag then she told me to go bring my cousins in for dinner. "They love you, Michael," she shouted as I headed out the back door.

Past a line of trees behind the house, I found Ted collapsed into a tire swing, the two chains dropping from the tall spruce above him twisted so tight he appeared trapped and hung.

From where he knelt in the sand with a toy dump truck,

eight-year-old Danny jumped to his feet. He ran to me and threw his arms around my waist. "Mike, Mike, Psych, Psych, Psycho." He giggled then punched me in the gut.

I got him in a headlock, brushed his head with my knuckle, and pushed him away from me. "Good to see you, too, Jerkface."

Ted dragged his feet to stop the swing. "Hey, Mike, did you know my dad chopped heads off in Korea." He was three years older than his brother, his face smeared in freckles, nose sun-burnt and he'd had a crew cut since I saw him last.

"Did not," shouted Danny and stomped towards the swing. Ted pushed his feet into the ground, raised his knees to his chest, spun in a blur of chain and boy, then with a hoot, slammed into Danny who fell to the ground, scrambled to his feet and threw himself at Ted, his hands a pinwheel of fists. Ted kneed him in the gut and Danny staggered back, doubled over, then came at him again.

"Fuck off, Danny," shouted Ted, and swung for him but missed.

I grabbed Danny and told him to smarten up.

He stuck out his tongue, pushed me away and ran through the trees.

Ted walked beside me back to the house. "He's spoiled."

"Whatever," I said. "Drop it, Ted."

We were quiet until the house was in sight.

"It's true about my dad. I heard him tell Chubby," said Ted.

"People say stupid things when they're drunk."

"I been drunk."

"You're a liar."

"You been drunk?"

"Not interested."

"Big suck."

I grabbed his arms and twisted them behind his

back. "Promise you won't talk to me anymore, and I'll let you go."

Back at the house, after asking where Danny was, Mary told Ted to pull his lip in and help me set the table. Roy stood in the kitchen doorway watching her bend over the oven. Her face flushed from the heat, she laughed as she told him about the grocery boy who'd dropped a row of soup cans on his foot when he was getting one down for her today. "Clumsy kid looked like he was going to start bawling."

Eyes fixed on her buttocks, Roy held a can of Lucky Lager in one hand and dangled a cigarette from his mouth. Danny burst into the room between his dad's legs, giggling and rolling on the floor. Roy put his beer on the counter, grabbed him by the shoulders and pulled him to his feet. "Whoa, Danny Boy." He turned Danny to face him and stuck out his stomach. "Come on Slugger, put it there." The cigarette in his mouth jerked up and down as he spoke.

Danny giggled while his tiny fists ricocheted off his father's belly.

"Can't even feel it. Harder, harder."

"Let me try," said Ted, dropping a pile of knives on the table and colliding with Mary, who held a steaming platter of chicken. "Ted," she shouted.

"Hey, hey, hey. Settle down, Ted," shouted Roy.

Ted stood squarely in front of Roy—the top of his head coming to his father's shoulders—his eyes sparking.

"Sit down," said Uncle Roy.

The evening air was heavy and little in the way of freshness moved between the two open doors. The family assembled at the table.

"We're going to have a house as big as my sister's one day, aren't we Roy," said Mary through a mouthful of mashed potatoes.

"Anything for you, Darling," said Roy. He swigged his beer and licked his lips, gazing across the table at his wife.

"With a swimming pool, a big swimming pool," said Danny, bouncing on his chair.

"You don't need a swimming pool; you got a lake right across the road," said Ted.

"Ah, Honey," laughed Mary. "Daddy'll build a big heart-shaped one just for you." She leaned over and kissed Danny on the lips. Danny flung his arms around her neck.

Roy rolled his eyes, tapped his fingernails on his can of Lucky. "I'm with Ted on this one," he said, winking at me.

Beside me, Ted sat up straight. "Dad's with me, Danny."

The next night, soon after Mary left for work, Chubby and Roy went to the legion. I made the boys and me hotdogs. After dinner, they bugged me to play Monopoly, which I've always hated, so I talked them into a game of hide-and-seek instead.

Outside, a pale sky domed a darkening forest and the smell of skunk cabbage pinched the air. We made the picnic table home base. I covered my eyes and began to count. As soon as the boys were out of sight, I went back into the house and locked both doors. On the kitchen counter, flies buzzed above the leftover wieners. I didn't expect Mary for an hour and Roy likely wouldn't be home until after midnight. I picked up the phone and tried to call my friend in Nanaimo, but when the operator came on and asked what number I was calling from, I hung up. I dug my book out of my bag. I was reading *Stranger in a Strange Land*, a story about an Earth kid raised by Martians who returns to Earth. It was silent outside and after about ten minutes, when I'd expected Danny to be banging on the door and he wasn't, I went out on the porch to check. Bats flitted from tree to tree in the empty yard. Then I heard voices coming from the start of the path that led to the Legion. Out of the dusk from between the trees came the tall bent figure of Roy with Danny hanging like a slain animal from his shoulder, except that his feet were kicking at Roy's chest and he was hollering between giggles, "Daddy, put me down."

"I bagged me a wild pig. We got us supper, Chubby," slurred Roy.

Chubby, a man half Roy's height, his fat belly hanging over his brass belt buckle, trailed behind them. In the sickly yellow light of the porch, he held out his hand to me. It was limp and damp. "You're Adele's boy." A tiny mouth sunk deep into his cheeks. "Your Auntie Mary will be happy I got him home before too late." He poked his thumb in Roy's direction and snorted.

Roy lowered Danny to the ground. "I scared my dad. He came down the path and I jumped out and scared him," said Danny.

"Where's Ted?" I asked.

"Go look for him," said Danny.

"We'll find him, Slugger," said Roy. He lifted Danny to his shoulders and they went around the front of the house. Chubby went inside and came out with two beers. I headed towards the woods where the trees were now dark silhouettes. Just then, Ted bolted from the other side of the house and ran toward the picnic table. "Home Free," he shouted, pounding the table with his fists.

Danny and Roy came around the side of the house, and Roy lifted Danny off his shoulders. "Get him, Tiger," he said. Danny rammed into Ted's back and both boys dropped to the ground in a snarl of feet and fist.

"Get to your feet, soldiers," said Roy. "Settle this like men. Sit down and face each other." He swayed back and forth. The boys scrambled to either side of the picnic table. "Let's do this fair and square. I call an arm wrestle."

"I don't want to," said Ted, rubbing his elbow after the tousle with Danny.

"Shut up, soldier." Roy lifted his head to the sky, chugged the last of the beer, and tossed the empty bottle across the grass.

"How about a wager?" said Chubby.

Roy grinned, then settled his hands on Danny's shoulders. "Ten bucks on my man here."

Chubby whistled. "Alright, then. Teddy, I'm counting on you, son."

Ted bit his bottom lip and dropped his elbow on the table. He grabbed Danny's hand. Danny leaned across the table and barred his teeth, then laughed. But Danny knew what his brother didn't know, that Ted was stronger than him. It took Ted seconds to push Danny's forearm into the picnic table with a loud thunk.

Ted's eyes lit up as they sought his father's.

"You gonna take that, Danny Boy," said Roy between his teeth. He shoved his younger son's shoulder and Danny scrambled away from the picnic table with a loud screech. Ted sprinted toward the house, but Danny overtook him and leaped on his back. Ted shook him off, grabbed him and put him in a headlock. Danny howled, twisted away and kicked Ted hard in the crotch.

"That-a-boy, get him, Danny, get him." Roy shouted.

My memory gets murky here, and I'm not sure who said what, but I retain an image of grown men slamming their fists in the thick dusk, and urging on violence: Uncle Roy's lurching drawl and Chubby's low snickering. Ted doubled over and shielding his face from a frenzy of fists. Danny springing away from his brother, bending to the ground and charging, a screech like a wild animal coming from his mouth. Danny heaving his body over and over into Ted's fists and his feet, both of them scraped and bloody with torn clothes. Ted in a heap gasping for breath. Danny's fingers bent like claws going for his brother's eyes. Ray shoving his youngest son again and again into his eldest son. In my memory, Danny has morphed from my bratty eight-year-old cousin into a frenzied red-faced, fist-flying beast. A creature born of his father.

I should have done something to stop it, but I was a kid; I didn't know how to go up against a guy like Roy. Truth is, I still don't. Back then, I stood frozen to the spot until I thought I was going to be sick, then I looked away. Across the road a dark mass of trees concealed the lake.

Seconds later, headlights bounced up the drive. Mary's car.

Roy grabbed Danny by his shirt collar. "Whoa, Tiger." With his other hand, he yanked his older son up by the arm. "Boys, go clean yourselves up."

They stumbled toward the porch. Both were smeared in dirt. Blood bubbled from Ted's nostrils and muddy tears traced his cheeks. As he passed me, I touched his elbow and tried to catch his eye. Without looking, he pushed my hand away. Danny followed, licking his bloodied fist.

That night from the room I shared with the boys I heard the angry pitch of Mary's voice through the bedroom door. I'd seen her give Roy hell many times and he took it, though he'd turn around the next day and do whatever it was he'd done to get her upset in the first place.

As I was drifting off, her voice came through the bedroom door. The fridge opened in the kitchen "Men do things with their sons—you do nothing... it doesn't have to be fishing. Something you can teach them. They want to do things with you—something that you like to do." Her voice grew softer, and then there was laughter.

She came into the room sometime in the middle of the night, beer-breathed and wafts of perfume. Danny had curled up on the floor next to me. She lifted him into his bed, gently, so he stayed asleep. After tucking him in she kneeled beside Ted, unwound the blanket from his face, and kissed him. He stirred in his sleep and turned away from her.

Mary was subdued the next morning. "Take them to the lake," she said.

The sun shone in a blue sky, and it was already hot. We crossed the highway between traffic and descended the short path between the trees to the beach. We climbed up onto a rocky bank, a perfect place to dive and stretch out in the sun. The boys dropped their towels and with a yelp cannon-balled off the edge, disappeared underwater. Then the lake rippled and stilled as if they'd never been there. Seconds ticked by before they burst onto the surface, a blur of arms and legs, wet faces and shouts.

Ted thrust his body away from the shore in a perfect crawl toward the middle of the lake, indifferent to the increasing depth beneath him. I wished his father could have seen him then, moving steadily forward in the same way he would one day leave that place. Danny paddled near shore, disappearing underwater then reappearing, quiet now, watching his brother.

"I'm going to swim like Ted one day, Mike."

"Yeah."

He leaned against the rock, half-in and half-out, his pale chest glistening, a shiny curl drooping over one eye.

"When my body moves the water out of the way, where does the water go?"

"It's displaced."

"You mean it disappears?"

I sat up and shrugged. "It's still there, it just goes somewhere else, kind of spreads out, if you know what I mean."

He sighed and slid beneath the surface.

The sun's warmth and the rising heat from the rock soothed the shock from the night before. The morning air sparked with light. The water, with all the force of a promise, carried Ted and held Danny.

A wisp of a cloud crossed the sun. Ted was a dot far from shore and Danny, as he climbed up the rocks, slipped, then recovered.

"Ted," I yelled. "Don't go out too far. Danny, be careful, those rocks are slippery."

There was no reason to leave the lake until late in the afternoon when we got hungry. We returned, relaxed and sun-soaked, up the path and across the highway. Danny's skin had bronzed in the sun and Ted's face was massed with freckles. They each looped an arm into mine, as we waited to cross the highway. Chubby's truck came around the corner with Uncle Roy on the passenger's side. Chubby honked the horn, pulled in at the bottom of the driveway and stopped. We jumped into the back and rode up to the house. The truck hadn't come to a full stop when Roy jumped out. I'd never seen him so animated, not drunk, just excited. He rushed around to the back, and dropped the tailgate. "Hey, boys, Daddy's got a present for you and a surprise for Mommy."

"What is it, Daddy?" Danny climbed onto Roy's back.

Roy held his hand toward Ted. "Come on, Son."

Ted drew back.

"Come on." Roy grabbed him and lifted him out of the truck. He reached past him for a long narrow box that was mixed in with various tools and a spare tire.

"Where's Aunt Mary?" I asked, as I got down from the truck.

"Groceries. She'll be back soon."

"Hiya Mike." Chubby held two cans of beer. "Want one?"

"No," I said, and turned to join Roy and the boys at the picnic table. From behind me came a sucking and a hissing sound. Chubby handed a beer to Roy.

While Roy cut the box open with a pocket knife, Danny clamoured around him, full of questions. Ted stood with his arms crossed, tapping his foot and biting his lip. The cardboard dropped away to reveal two slender wooden rifles.

"Wow," said Danny, reaching for one. His dad slapped his hand away. "Wait."

"Guns?" said Ted, his eyes wide.

"Well, they sure's hell aren't Barbies, are they?" said Roy. They're not going to hurt you." He swung the gun to his shoulder and aimed it toward the lake. "You didn't know your dad was a master marksman during the war, did you?" He squinted his eye and looked through the sight, his body taut.

Ted shook his head, and Danny ran around the table. "Let me try, let me try."

"Slow down, Slugger. Daddy is going to teach you how to do this right. These aren't toys. We're going to go target practicing, father and sons. It's going to make your mom so happy." He downed half his beer. "Your poor mom deserves to be happy, don't you think. And in the meantime, we're going to have fun."

That last time I saw Danny, he led his father and brother along with Chubby into the forest, his head held high with the gun that was half the length of his body resting its butt end in the palm of his hand. His dark head of curls bounced in time with the ceaseless burbling of his voice and his eyes shone with a blinding light.

Sitting on the wharf thirty years later, I sip cold coffee, dump out the remains, and scrunch the cup in my hand.

The water beneath the boards trembles in the wind coming off the lake. In the car, driving north, I wonder what Danny would have been like had he lived: a drinker like his father or maybe worse, a man made unremarkable from life's wear and tear.

My parents came for me the day after the accident. That's what we called it: an accident. It was my mom who found Ted curled like a wood bug in the forest near where the day before he'd shot his brother.

Ted left home at sixteen and now owns a company that takes out huge sections of the rainforest in Bolivia: a logger like his daddy. My father called him a successful man.

I thought the memory was gone, but it's fresh, like it happened yesterday: the three of us waiting on the side of the highway for a break in traffic: bathing suits under our t-shirts and towels draped around our necks, my cousins daring one another to make the crossing in sight of an oncoming car. I can still feel the tension in those moments: looking first in one direction then in the other, the boys impatient at my side, the taste of dust in my mouth, the pockmarked pavement and smell of exhaust. And on the other side, the glimmer and sparkle of the blue lake through the trees.

Her Father's Jilted Lover

The sky above Becher Bay, overcast again, spits and sputters like a car that can't quite get started. Hoping the fresh air will relieve her migraine, Marilee steps out of the travel trailer onto the deck, but the air is so big it nearly knocks her over. The ocean waves terrorize one another and the chill drills her head and seizes her body. A quick retreat inside and the wind, as if glad to be rid of her, grabs the door and slams it hard.

The propane furnace fouls the air with its oily breath, exhales a mould-sticky dust. Hoodie pulled tight over her head and blanket around her shoulders, Marilee drops to the floor and folds her legs into a lotus position. She strokes the mala beads on her wrist while reciting OM AH HUM seven times, tries to picture a soft white light soothing the migraine but sees instead a wedge of metal lodged along the ridge of her eyebrows.

She tries again. Her mind is muddled, undecided, but her body knows what it wants. Coffee, which she hasn't had in two days. *Inhale, exhale.* Her father is an idiot. He won't replace the old furnace, probably doesn't even notice it's broken. *Buddha mind, loving-kindness.* The fumes could asphyxiate her and no one would find her for days. *Purify the mind, the body.* She is alone for the first time in her life. No computer, no phone. She is doing this to herself—cutting herself off. Her cellphone and laptop, buried in a box at her mother's house an hour and a half away. *Follow the breath.* Twenty-five, and all Marilee has accumulated fits into six cardboard boxes stored at her mother's house. If only her poverty, such as it is, were motivated by a desire for non-attachment. Virtue. *Cool white light.* Isn't poverty relative? Doesn't she have a cellphone while millions don't even have food? It was dangerous not to bring her cellphone. What if she falls down the bank and breaks her leg? Nobody comes to this part of the campground. It's why her father chose it, of course. *Watch the thoughts drift by.*

She envisions her father's dingy trailer as a clammy cave, herself a bodhisattva wrapped in saffron. But even as her breath softens into an even rhythm she knows she doesn't have the fortitude for enlightment. It's the small things she wants, the tangibles like everyone else. Right now, for example, she wants coffee, something to constrict the brain's blood vessels, something to squeeze out the pain. *Follow the breath.* Something quick. When the headache is gone, it will be some other thing she wants, some fleeting remedy for the most minor of discomforts—a quick fix, a temporary entertainment.

The truth is she is weak. *Don't attach to negative thoughts.* She squirms at the sound of the wind whining through a crack in the window. *Follow the breath.* If death were a sound, it would be wind off the ocean. She doesn't usually think about death even though the Buddhist monk at the community centre taught them that contemplating death helps them to appreciate its opposite.

Death rhymes with breath, and aren't they two ends of the continuum. Death and breath: a juxtaposition.

Her mind scurries toward this thought, or not the thought itself but the profundity of her mind, its deep basal canyons. Is this what a realization feels like? *Death rhymes with breath.* Then she wonders if a moment of realization might be something like orgasm. She does feel a stirring in her pelvic area.

And the moment collapses and here she is in a smelly trailer with a migraine, and at the memory of her father's pot stash in the cupboards above the table, her eyes pop open. A low frustrated wail at the door and it's as if she's out there on the wind, jerked this way and that.

She was five years old the first time her parents brought her to Beecher Bay where her father had leased a spot far out on a rocky promontory. That summer, moss as green as limes covered the rocks in the shade of the Arbutus trees and every morning the mist dissipated off a sun-pricked ocean and every night she lay between her parents on the rocks looking to the stars and imagining a distant meadow of tiny flowers above her head.

Marilee stands on a chair and peers deep into the back of the cupboard above the stove for a bag of pot, a solitary joint, even a bit of resin. She sniffs and reaches into the empty space, turns up only a mound of crumbs crawly with ants and a can of sardines. Her father used to leave sugar in plastic containers, a jar of instant coffee, peanut butter, provisions in anticipation of the next visit. She drops into the chair— stones ping inside her skull: a dismal rattle in her head.

After a few years, it was usually her father and Marilee who spent a week or two at the beach in the summer and occasional weekends during the rest of the year. Marilee's mother was busy getting a law degree then building a career, and this threw father and daughter together. They played Crazy Eights and explored the beach; on rare hot days, Marilee swam while he stood ankle deep near the shore, a goose-pimpled pale-skinned prairie boy, beguiled and defeated by the sea.

When her parents split three years ago, her father moved to the beach and every few weeks Marilee drove out to visit him. When she arrived, she usually found him standing outside waiting. He'd walk toward the car as she pulled into the drive. She'd still be turning off the ignition while he opened the door. "How's she running?" he'd say, even before saying hello, as if it were the car he'd been waiting for. He'd talk about the muffler, the timing, did she remember to get a tune up. He'd lift the hood, a reason not to look at her, and with his face lowered he'd list what he'd gotten in for dinner: spot prawns, fresh salmon, organic broccoli from the farm down the road and sometimes a cake he'd made himself. He never found anything wrong with the car.

On clear nights they watched the sky and shared a joint while telling each other that it helped them sleep. One time, Marilee said it wasn't right that her mother had sold all the furniture he'd built for the family.

A thin joint dangled between his lips, the lit end bobbing like a tiny beacon in the dark. He dropped his head back, and inhaled. Holding the smoke in his lungs so that his voice was strained he said, "Memory settles into wood and your mother prefers the next thing. She doesn't look back in the way wood wants you to. She has her reasons." He never asked about her mother though Marilee liked to imagine that he missed her. For such a long time there was no one, not even friends in his life.

And then two months ago when Marilee was working the afternoon shift, her father walked into Starbucks holding the hand of a woman thin as paper, a cutout doll he introduced as Nancy.

"Pleased to meet you," said Nancy, her voice like vapour, as she entwined her fingers in a near-prayer gesture.

Marilee, pretending she didn't hear, flipped a switch on the espresso machine, but then when she saw Nancy startle at the machine's sudden sputtering, she felt over-large in proximity to the woman's delicate limbs, and cruel. "Hi," she said, "sorry, a bit busy here."

Nancy looked around; the place was empty.

"Was, I meant," said Marilee. "Busy, an hour ago. It's up and it's down, you know."

"We can come back," said her Dad.

"No, I can take a break. No prob. Let me make you something."

Her father tilted his head toward Nancy, his lips and eyes smiling. She ordered a caramel frapuchhino. Marilee scrimped on Nancy's caramel.

The metal legs of the chairs scraped the tile floor as all three sat down. It was raining outside and droplets of water skittered down Nancy's blonde hair. At first, they sipped their coffee in silence while the machines burbled behind the counter. Her father explained that he had met Nancy in the office of the construction company where he now worked. Marilee found herself comparing Nancy to her mother, something she'd told herself she wouldn't do when the time came. She decided that Nancy's hand on her father's knee under the table was *inappropriate*. *Inappropriate* and *juvenile*, two of Marilee's mother's favorite adjectives. Marilee imagined Nancy and her father talking when he went into the office every second Friday to pick up his pay cheque. They would have talked about banal things: the weather, the price of gas—a banality that her father would have found comforting after her mother. And Nancy would have noticed his big hands, his gentle voice, perhaps. Why hadn't her father warned her about Nancy? Marilee sipped her double Americano, her Dad slurped his coffee and Nancy stared at hers as if it was something she'd never encountered before.

"Did Dad tell you he used to make furniture when we lived out Ivy Road? He had a big workshop and one time he let me run the skill saw. Mistake. Nearly cut my hand off, blood everywhere, me screaming bloody murder. We thought I was going to lose my finger. I still have the scar." She held up her index finger and the puckered skin around the knuckle shone under the fluorescents. "I just might get a tattoo there. Don't know what of though." For a second, the way Nancy leaned towards her and blinked, her eyelashes caked in mascara, Marilee was afraid that she might offer a suggestion: a mermaid or a unicorn, something like that.

"It wasn't that bad," said Marilee's father, shifting in his chair.

"Careless. He's just a bit careless, and I guess I've inherited that from him."

Nancy's hands were aflutter, her mouth conjuring a smile. "I'm sure he was good at woodworking."

"Talented, yes," said Marilee and looked deeply into her double Americano. He'd never been far from her and her mother, working in the shop out back and even now after the break-up—they always knew where he was, like coordinates on a map you could get a fix on: her father in his workshop or at the beach. For awhile, before her mother sold, he'd drive into town and work at the house in his shop. Then came the day when he got a job at a construction company and he didn't come in anymore. He was building houses in a new subdivision near the beach; he said he didn't like the way they'd stripped the land of the trees. Why hadn't she heard about Nancy?

"Yes, I'm sure he was very good," said Nancy again, brushing a limp strand of hair behind her shoulder in a gesture that confirmed for Marilee that this girlfriend would allow her father to be less than he was, that his goodness was now in the past.

"I don't know about 'good' said her father. I never made much of a living at it." He breathed noisily in through his nose and glanced outside. "I'm making a decent wage now. I've told you that, Marilee. You bringing this up so I won't ask about school?" He grinned. She and he had taken to this reversal of roles. They'd go back and forth being the parent. It was necessary that Nancy knew this. Their view through the Starbucks massive window was a shopping mall parking lot grayed with rain.

"You have talent. Don't waste it." Marilee didn't like that she heard her mother's voice in her own.

"Chill, Marilee."

"You've always told me to follow my heart." Her voice tightened, drove upward.

Nancy rubbed her pale hand along his thigh and fixed her gaze on Marilee. "He's moving into town," she said, her voice like dandelion seeds detonating.

In the cupboard above the table Marilee forages for pot and for coffee, sniffs like an animal. She rifles through a jumble of board games in broken boxes, loose jigsaw pieces, old bills. She finds a book: *Mushroom Picking in the Pacific Northwest*. She'd once bought her father a book on trees, but she doubts he ever looked at it; he isn't a reader. A man who likes to touch and smell and see has no need to name things. When she was a girl, he would point to two trees and tell her to notice their differences: *use your eyes, your nose, your fingertips*. It was not the names he wanted her to know, it was the tree.

Neither of her parents had ever shown any interest in foraging. Food was something purchased at a grocery store, though Marilee recalled her mother's herb phase. One summer they'd planted rosemary, oregano, thyme, dill and mint in the sunniest corner of the yard. Interest waned and

Marilee came to correlate the gradual neglect of the herb garden—the plants turning unruly and bitter—with the deterioration of her parent's marriage. Her mother's fondness for herbs gave way to a preference for drought-tolerant shrubs and green lawns. Her father preferred the beach.

A week after meeting Nancy, Marilee had driven the six boxes over to her mother's house. In her mother's kitchen, their voices ricocheted off granite and stainless steel surfaces. Like a bird to its perch, her mother clung to the barstool alone at the island. Marilee knew it wasn't easy for her to watch her daughter pass by the kitchen and through the basement door, cardboard boxes pressed against her chest. Her refusal to help Marilee hump the six boxes down the stairs was her way of communicating her disapproval, a missive she considered a necessary aspect of love. She wanted Marilee to understand that *there wouldn't always be someone around to bale her out.*

The newspaper was open to the crossword on the counter in front of her mother. On the last trip downstairs as Marilee passed the open door, her mother said, "Line from the heart."

Marilee's own heart expanded and contracted like a balloon—she was not a fit girl. "How many letters?" she was able to gasp.

Her mother looked up and sighed. "Put it down and I'll get it later."

Marilee lowered the box to the floor in the hallway and in the kitchen she climbed onto a stool; they were high and dangerous in her mother's kitchen.

"Five," said her mother, returning to the crossword.

"It starts with an A, I think."

"No, that's artery."

"Aorta."

Her mother nodded and wrote the word into the little

squares. She removed her glasses and rubbed her eyes. "What happened with the boy?"

"He wasn't exactly a boy."

"Manner of speaking."

Her mother had met Wilf once and liked him because he had direction. She likes direction in the way that some mothers like a pleasant manner.

"We fought."

"Couples do. It must have been a bad one."

"Not really. I wanted chickens and he didn't."

"I didn't think you ate meat, and Marilee, that seems trivial."

"I wanted them for the eggs, for the backyard."

"You wanted chickens in the backyard."

"Yes, urban chickens, it's legal now."

"This broke up your relationship." Her mother slid off the stool, stood with her arms crossed.

"Really, it was the flowers he brought me after the fight."

Her mother shook her head slowly. "I'm afraid I'm not following you."

"They were roses."

"Yes."

"Roses are cliché, Mom."

"You broke up over roses and chickens."

"People have broken up over less."

Her mother's eyes were almost the same green as her countertop. She sat down with another sigh and ran her hands through her hair. "Marilee, life is cliché. There's no escaping it."

What Marilee wouldn't tell her mother was that she'd dropped her courses, all of them, in mid-February, that she'd been living on her Starbucks salary in a student house where conversations concerning macroeconomics and pedagogical theories bellowed incomprehensibly around her, that there was something lewd in the way boney-elbowed Wilf and pudgy Madeline, all bulges in her Lululemons, spit unknowingly from the corners of their mouths at one another in their excited polemics. It didn't surprise her to hear that Madeline had moved into Wilf's room two weeks after Marilee moved out.

Her mother stood again and crossed the expanse of her kitchen to pick up the kettle. She filled it with water and plugged it into the wall. "What now?" The words came out on a click of the tongue.

"I'm meeting Tammy for lunch."

"I meant where are you going to live, how is your financial situation, that sort of thing."

"I thought... "

"That you would stay here."

"Temporarily."

Her mother cleared her throat and glanced at the clock.

"I'm looking for a better job," said Marilee. "It wouldn't be long."

"School?"

"I'm finished. It's almost May now."

"What about summer session? This is your last year, Marilee. You're almost twenty-six. I had my undergrad when I was twenty-one."

"I had a couple of false starts."

Her mother rested her chin in her hands and her elbows on the counter. The kettle gasped. "I worry that maybe it was the divorce, that it was harder on you than I thought. It's just that you weren't a child when we split."

Marilee squirmed, looked at the clock. "It's not your fault Mom, the way I am. I would have been this way, anyway. Even if you and Dad had stayed together."

"What way?"

"Well, you know. Twenty-five, half-educated, half-employed. Seeking enlightenment."

"I'm not saying you're a certain 'way'." Then she said sometimes you have to be cruel to be kind. Another cliché. This was her reasoning behind not allowing Marilee to move back home. "Your father has always forced me to be the tough cop." She twisted her legs around the metal stool in her hollow clutter-free kitchen.

"I understand," said Marilee, though this pained her mother, who was more comfortable with adversity.

"Can you get more hours at work?"

"I'm looking for something else. Don't worry."

"I'm not. It's not that you are not capable."

It's often how her mother compliments, encourages Marilee: with double negatives.

Her father offered the trailer and reminded Marilee that she never had to ask. He didn't understand that it was a last resort. He thought Marilee loved the beach in the same way she had when she was a little girl. The truth was the trailer was an hour and a half out of town, and though her friend Sarah had said she could stay at her apartment, Sarah had just moved in with Jake. Marilee knew she'd feel inadequate around all the pairs of things: the two sets of keys hanging by the door, the different coloured toothbrushes, his hiking boots dwarfing hers, the blue MEC windbreaker hanging beside the smaller mauve MEC windbreaker.

She packed a few clothes and two books: *How to Meditate* and *What The Buddha Said*. She stopped at a market and bought vegetables, brown rice and quinoa. She would detoxify her body and get in touch with her very subtle being. Change her deluded mind. After a week, she would collect her laptop and cellphone, move in with Sarah and Jake until she could find an apartment and a decent job. She would develop intention, imbue ambition with a pure motivation: perhaps work towards the liberation of Tibetan monks or start a xeriscaping movement on Vancouver Island. She would think in the future tense.

Marilee rubs the place where it hurts the most, just above the eyes. She flips through the book past glossy coloured photographs of mushrooms with their convoluted folded flesh, in dull browns, blues and reds. A dried mushroom tarred black and rough like a scab drops on her lap from between the pages. She pinches it between her fingers and searches for its likeness in the photographs on the open page. *A black relative of the chanterelle, Craterellus cornucopioides, is called "the trumpet of death," and yet it is not poisonous.*

The mushroom between her fingers was, in fact, shaped like a tiny, flattened trumpet. *Its dark cap, gray underside, and its habit of growing in dark places under shrubs make this secretive mushroom a challenge to find.*

Marilee flips to the inside cover and scans for a signature. Could it have been the vacuous Nancy who gave her father the mushroom book? No clues. Nancy is surely more the petunia type. Marilee rubs the Trumpet of Death between her fingers and wonders fleetingly what might happen if she were to smoke it and then disgusted with herself, rolls her eyes and shoves the book back into the cupboard.

She pulls on her boots and drags a sweater over her hoodie. No matter how many sweaters you wear on this beach, you brace yourself: the wind, the damp. She shuts the door behind her and steps down the two metal steps to the wooden deck, her shoulders hunched toward her ears. The sky's bone-coloured pall forces her to squint and sends a sharp pain up one side of her head. A walk will help. With her sunglasses on, the sea and the forest dull to amber. The wind, no longer fierce, shushes the treetops and the waves roll half-heartedly. She steps between arbutus across a mound of mossy stone and descends onto a dirt path that traces the shoreline through undergrowth in the forest. The path leads out of the campground and in behind some local houses for three or four kilometres to the next bay. On a rise at the root mound of a lone maple, a cluster of white flowers wrapped in mottled green leaves lean their bright heads toward the earth. She stoops to have a better look.

"Fawn lilies," says a voice behind her.

Marilee spins around, one hand on the ground. A large woman leans forward and to one side with her forearms crossed and each hand cupped over the handle of a cane carved in the likeness of a raven, its head located beneath the woman's fingers, it's beak pointed at Marilee.

"A late bloomer, that one. Seed sits in the earth for years and when it finally shows up, it insists on being one of the first ones awake in these dark woods every spring. Pretty aren't they?"

"They're fragile looking," says Marilee, standing up.

"Don't let them fool you. You Marilee?"

"Yes, how did you know?"

"You look like your father." A mass of grey hair stretched tightly across a mountain of a head gathers into a ponytail that falls to the woman's waist. One hip under her sweat pants is higher than the other.

"Do you know him? Do you live in the campground?"

"No, I live a few minutes down the trail. I'm Sunny." She leans on one cane and holds out her hand. Marilee sees that if this strange woman were to stand straight up she would loom by at least a foot over herself. What a burden to haul that mass of flesh and bone around from morning until night.

"Don't suppose he ever mentioned me," says Sunny.

Marilee knows that it's not a question, that the twisted giantess doesn't want an answer. She takes the fleshy hand. "Name's Marilee, but you know that."

"Dan often talked fondly of you."

Dan—she rarely hears people call him that—never mentioned Sunny: a friend, a woman at the beach even. She has an uneasy sense that Sunny doesn't live down the trail, but has morphed supernaturally from the rough bark of trees.

"You looking after his place?" asks Sunny.

"Well, no, not exactly. I'm staying here for a bit, between jobs."

"You're a barista, so your father says."

"I am? Is that what he calls me? I guess. Yah, I make coffee for a living, at least I did." Marilee removes her sunglasses and rubs her forehead.

"Headache?"

"Kind of. Well, yah, migraine. I get migraines."

"Like your father."

"How do you know so much about him?"

"Let's just say." The woman tips her head toward the tops of the trees and then levels her dark eyes on Marilee. "We fucked."

Marilee steps back and her toe catches on a protruding rock. She stumbles and rights herself. No one has ever said that to her before about her father.

"You learn a lot about a person that way," says Sunny, apparently non-plussed by Marilee's near-tumble.

"I guess."

"He helped me out. You can see I'm gimped. 80% of the brain is water and in my case, even more. You've heard the expression *water on the brain* meant as an insult, but don't kid yourself, some smart people have water on the brain. Believe me, I know lots about lots of things and I don't need Google. I don't even have a goddamned computer. You look like hell, but I want to tell you something. You haven't had a headache till you've had your brain swelled up. Now that's a headache. People die."

"You fucked."

"Is that a question?" Sunny lifts her eyebrows causing lines like craters to appear in the skin on her forehead. Marilee imagines apocalyptic surgeries, fleshy scars on the head of the giantess. She's heard of hydrocephalus.

"Well, no, not exactly a question, I guess."

"You think your daddy doesn't have a dick."

Marilee shakes her head and puts her glasses back on. Sunny turns amber.

"Now then, I think we're off to a bad start." Sunny propels her body in a half-circle with the aid of her canes and begins to shuffle and sway down the path in the direction Marilee assumes she came. On her back she carries a woven basket rigged with straps so it sits on her shoulders. She leaves a blur of dirt behind her, like a slug trail. What an ugly woman she is, this one with her hunched and twisted spine, her cedar red skin. Some troll from the woods. Marilee might have been in one of those terrifying fairy tales where an innocent child is about to get eaten.

"In case you're wondering, I'm not going to fatten you up and eat you," Sunny hollers over her shoulder. Marilee thinks she hears the woman's voice breaking as if she's going to cry.

A mist has severed the trees. Marilee follows Sunny. She tries not to think of her father kissing the grotesque woman or worse, lying naked with her. She doesn't ever recall seeing him kiss her own mother, and yet it must have happened. She likes to imagine they were once in love, though she's never been herself.

"It's going to rain," says Sunny. Her voice is big in the dim woods.

"I thought we were in a rain shadow here. It seems like it's going to rain but it never actually does."

"How do you think these trees got so big? Of course it rains. Just because you don't see it doesn't mean it doesn't happen. The evidence is all around you." Sunny's voice turns sing-song and breathless.

Why is Marilee following this woman? Because this is what Marilee does. She walks into situations without planning or thinking; for example, when she feels she may have dropped into a migraine-induced nightmare, she keeps walking.

The trees thin and the path weaves between a thicket of Devil's club that reach their monstrous spiny leaves skyward and press against the outside walls of a well-camouflaged cabin with a small covered porch. On either side of the door sit two wicker chairs stained black from mould.

"Take a load off," says Sunny and goes through the door.

The rain begins to fall, slow at first and then with increasing intensity. Marilee, just out of the deluge sits in one of the chairs and breathes in the fleshy stench of mould; her stomach roils. Rain slides off the trees and there is a steady pounding on the earth. Just beyond the bush in front of the house she sees a gravel road. Her clothes, hair, even her skin are damp. From the house comes the sound of running water, the clank of a kettle. Sunny appears on the porch. No canes now, she heaves and shuffles away from the house down a narrow trail. She wears gardening gloves and clutches a pair of small clippers. She reaches beneath a cluster of leaves and snips at the stem of the Devil's Club, takes away a short thorny stalk back into the house without saying a word.

"Your dad said you were a baby sometimes. Only child, I guess it's unavoidable," she shouts from inside. "Don't get me wrong. He loves you... too much, I think."

Marilee stares at the dense patch of Devil's Club. Surely, this woman will turn her into a frog or worse, cook her alive. It will be her father's fault for fucking her and what business does he have talking about Marilee to a stranger.

Sunny comes from the house carrying a tray with a teapot and two chipped mugs.

"Devil's Club Tea. It'll put hair on your chest." She places the tray on a round of firewood that serves as a table, pours a cup of bitter smelling greenish liquid and hands it to Marilee.

"Ah, no thanks."

Sunny settles into the other chair and says, "People been curing themselves of headaches with it for centuries, but if it's too good for you." She looks away and again Marilee detects a catch in her throat.

"It's made from Devil's Club?" asks Marilee after a moment.

"The stem. Your dad had it lots. How come he never told you?"

Marilee shrugs. The funny thing is she's beginning to understand how difficult it would be to explain Sunny, as if really she is the figment of a dream. Then again, was the giantess really some crazed stalker who, had her father not moved away from the beach, would have poisoned him? She glances at Sunny from the corner of her eye. Her flesh spills over the chair and her head lolls like a newborn's head on her neck. Her mouth is puckered into an O shape and a deep furrow above the bridge of her nose makes it look like she worries about things. Marilee feels guilty for imagining her naked father atop this mound of contorted flesh and for a moment she feels bad for Sunny. She sips the tea and when her mouth explodes with bitterness she spits it out.

Sunny laughs. "Baby."

"You drink it." Marilee says, jumping to her feet.

Sunny lifts Marilee's cup to her lips, tips and swallows. "It's an acquired taste."

The rain has stopped but a heavy mass of clouds sits not far above them.

"Want a pharmaceutical, an analgesic of the manufactured variety?" asks Sunny, her dark gaze gone over the Devil's club shrubbery out to the road.

"What have you got?"

"Everything from Celebrex to Percocet. What's your poison?"

"Marijuana."

"Got that too, your dad likes that stuff. He told me it would help me with the pain. Never smoked it before I met him. Works like a hot damn. Not all the time. Nothing works all the time. Wish life were that simple."

She shakes her big head and it makes Marilee think of the Newfoundland dog she had when she was a kid. Marilee stares at the other woman who stares into the mist-dripping trees. "How do you manage on your own?"

"Breaking news, Kid. That's the only way any of us manages." She's not so ugly when she smiles. She sits on the edge of her chair, a chunk of a woman whose slightest movement is an argument with her body. "I was born this way, in case you're wondering," she says.

Marilee smiles. "So was I, though my mother blames the way I am on my father."

The sky lets lose with a torrent of rain as Marilee walks through the woods back to her father's trailer. Exited birdsong surrounds her, and a musty cedar-tinged tang sharpens the air. She's at peace, and she doesn't know if it's from whatever her father's strange lover gave her or the spacey aftermath of a migraine. Random drops of rain fall through the trees' canopy and cool her forehead. She laughs at the thought she's been anointed. She's looking forward to spending the evening alone with herself.

Senanus Island

The pebble-searing sea startles Mandy awake. She leaps to her feet with the feeling something is wrong. She's always trusted her gut that way and sure enough, there, just offshore in the whitecaps, her escaped kayak bucks for joy. She swims toward the kayak with Pearce's voice nattering in her head. It's not like him not to come after her.

The wind switches off and she grabs at the kayak, runs her fingers along the fiberglass and eases it toward shore. She loves this boat. When she and Pearce bought hers and his as wedding gifts for one another they joked that they might call them *Effort 2*. Both were marrying for a second time. His had a gold-colored rudder. "Rooster tails," she'd teased him. In the end she dubbed her own, *My Tangerine Baby*. He'd grinned and trapped her in his eyes, the way he does. She loves that look. She loves how his eyes don't reveal his mood, how he keeps her guessing.

Back on the beach, she pulls the boat over the rocks and drops onto a flat sun-heated stone. After all these years, she's on Indian Island. It's what her parents called it before you weren't supposed to say *Indian*. Behind the marina, a jumble of condominiums interrupt the forest. On the other side of the inlet a highway skirts the edge of a mountain from which drifts the hum of traffic. In between there is tiny Indian Island and the water.

Four o'clock. She left him an hour and a half ago. Childish, the way they'd split off like that, their slick boats bouncing in opposite directions across the bay. Childish, the way she'd said, "Fuck you, Pearce," and dug her paddle deep, the weight of the whole ocean pushing against the blade. She faced away from him before the tears came. She never lets him see the tears.

"Mandy, calm down," he'd called, the wind shredding his words so that she wasn't sure if he'd said it at all.

She's forty-one, too old to be cursing out her husband, Pearce once told her. He'd say, "let's not fight," and this would make her want to fight more because she felt that he was trying to muzzle her. She'd get angry and he'd match her anger and rev it up. Mandy would let him go a bit wild and then she'd bring things down. She liked feeling in control that way, but hated the fall-out afterwards—the wasted hours and the shame.

She and Pearce have perfect days on the water. How many couples have perfect days? He'd taught her the right strokes, made her match the movement of his arms, the subtle twist in his body, how to slide along the surface of the ocean side-by-side. Once he'd towed her when she was too tired to go on and one night under a full moon he'd gathered oysters on the beach and pried them open with his Swiss army knife. He'd poured raw oysters down her throat and they became something savory and secret in her belly.

Maybe he's in the marina pub waiting for her. He's not a drinker like her first husband, but he can nurse a beer with the look of a man who considers himself ill-treated, the eyes narrow and small, eyebrows caving into one another. It's early September, and the sun will be dropping into the sea within a couple of hours. Something is wrong.

They've been married for three years now and it's hard with her son, and these weekends when Gerard is with his dad she tries to make her time alone with Pearce precious. Today is her fault. Why'd she have to bring it up? On the other hand, is it too much to ask that he talk to his stepson?

"I try. He hates me," Pearce had said.

They'd paddled a short way from the marina and were waiting for the Mill Bay ferry to get out of their path. A slight chop rocked the boats. She couldn't see his eyes through his sunglasses.

"He doesn't hate you. He's sixteen. Don't you remember being sixteen and finding out, hey, it's not like it's supposed to be."

He smacked the blade of his paddle on the surface of the water, distracted—how he gets. He can't sit still for long, is always fiddling in the kayak, leaning this way and that, spinning in circles, fiddling with the paddle. Sometimes he tries to do Eskimo rolls—over and over again—he gets obsessed. But he hasn't succeeded yet. He stopped. "And now what? You want *me* to solve your son's anger problem?"

It was that he'd said, "your son," not claiming his stepson, and therefore, in her mind, not claiming her. And it was the spit that came out of the side of his mouth.

Fuck you, Pearce.

She gets to her feet and faces the wall of trees along the bank. There's no path in sight, and yet she's certain it was this bay where her father dropped the anchor. Where they'd lowered themselves into the shallow water and her mother had passed them the camping gear and the food. There'd been a grassy meadow near the beach where she'd helped her father pitch the tent. It's still there, she's sure, somewhere in the trees. She wades through a mat of gumweed up the bank. At the top, she turns and scans the water for any sign of Pearce. It's not that he doesn't know where she is, though he's not landed here before. They've passed it enough times in kayaks on their way down the inlet. He always says, "We can't land on a First Nations burial ground." It's not that Pearce stands much on principle, except when it comes to the dead.

Mandy wants Pearce to be with her here on the island, to get how perfect it was with her family all those years ago, how she came from stock that could be perfect. Pearce had finally agreed.

Standing above the beach she closes her eyes and tries to bring back the musty smell of a canvas tent, the sizzle of bacon frying on the Coleman stove, the collapsing driftwood as it disintegrated in the fire after dark. She strains to hear in her memory her brother Brandon's high-pitched laughter. He was younger than her and copied everything she did. They fashioned bows and arrows from sticks and fishing line and played at killing cougars and pirates. On the island, unlike at home, Brandon and she weren't afraid of anything.

Pearce and she never talk about fear. Before they met, he paddled alone in the worst conditions and he never tells her not to paddle alone.

The underbrush thins as the trees get taller and the shade deepens. Mandy walks away from the shore, and it's not long before the forest opens up and she steps into a clearing, yellow with grass and sunshine. She's on the other side of the island. She smiles at the sudden memory of slithering on her belly through the deep dry grass with Brandon. And how her parents had been there, also on the ground, grass flattened beneath them. Her mother on her back with pale breasts rising into the sultry air, eyes closed and her father lowering himself onto her as if he were doing pushups: all around the buzzing of cicadas, somewhere the stink of animal excrement. And it had struck her as comical—her father's skinny buttocks and her mother's sighs. Brandon had cried out and Mandy slapped her hand over his mouth, dragged him to his feet and back into the forest. By the time they dropped out of earshot beneath the trees, Brandon's whimpering had pitched into tears, his cheeks damp and smeared with dirt. When she rolled on the ground giggling, he finally giggled, too. It was after this that Brandon came to understand like Mandy that his family was different on the water than at home.

At home there were nights when Brandon would come to her room and she would bury him in blankets, cover his ears. And in the morning something was broken: a lamp or a glass and the space between her parents—jittery with shame.

They were allowed to stay up late on the island. Their father would tell stories about the Indian people that were buried there, how when a boat sunk out on the bay or somebody drowned, it was the work of a ghost. Though her father had never said so, she'd always believed that as long as they didn't fight, they were safe from the Indian ghosts.

Mandy returns to the beach and drops onto the gravel. Behind her the tops of the firs are ramrod straight. The air is windless and the light is shifting into evening's purple hues. Even the gulls are quiet. She recognizes nothing. Pearce was right. There's nothing here for her, only the water endlessly circling the island. The ocean is flat now, so different from only an hour ago. She thinks every shape on the horizon is Pearce.

The sun has sunk on the other side of the island so that the trees and shoreline on her side cast long shadows. Her skin is covered in goose bumps. She pulls a fleece coat over her bathing suit, the life jacket and the sprayskirt.

Out on the water the light has given everything a brass finish and made the edges of rocks and trees as distinct as cedar carvings, the soft haze of the afternoon, gone. She squints into the setting sun and is able to make out the marina across the bay. It takes her forty minutes to make the crossing. The ocean's black surface smells cold. The ferry dock is empty.

That time on the island was the only time she recalls seeing her mother's bare breasts where, unbeknownst to anyone, cancer cells were dividing and multiplying. Her mother has been gone more years than Brandon. Her father lives on a boat in Florida with a woman Mandy's never met.

Her eye catches a movement, a violent flashing red light on the bank above the marina: an ambulance, people shouting and carrying a stretcher between them. On it is the shape of a man, or so she thinks, because it is too large to be a woman or a child.

Her immediate thought is to turn back to the island because surely by now Pearce is waiting for her, that he's there with the Indian ghosts, but she can't move, and it's dark.

On weekends when Gerard's dad comes to pick him up, Mandy goes somewhere in the house where she can avoid contact with her ex-husband.

In the dark she drifts toward shore until it's shallow enough for her to fumble her way out of the kayak. She walks up the ramp where she and Pearce carried the kayaks down earlier in the day. The light on the ambulance is off now and there's a murmur of voices. No one is in a hurry. She stops a short distance from the ambulance where a kayak with a gold rudder lies empty on its side. Pearce never uses his rudder. She can't control the kayak on her own, not like he can. She shivers in the cold. She can't control anything. Even her face is trembling now, twitching. It is so cold.

The man from the marina is by her side and asks her if she was the woman with Pearce. He knows she was, but he wants to be sure. "Seems he did one of those eskimo rolls and knocked himself out on wreckage from an old dock; flotsam, no one knows where it came from. Hell of a gash he took. He was hanging upside down, couldn't right himself. Terrible tragedy. We thought you were..."

"We got separated," she says, and thinks *Isn't that what people do*. She hasn't seen her brother for six years.

The man puts a blanket around her shoulders. It's weightless and without warmth—insubstantial as water.

This Karst Landscape

Mist, like an albino cat, hunched over the peak of the Golden Hinde, Vancouver Island's tallest mountain, descended into cottony balls, and fringed the lake. Tilde strode along the shore. Burt's eyes followed the jackknife of her legs, pale and sturdy as birch limbs. As she walked, she rubbed her short, sharp hair with a towel. She was clothed now in a t-shirt as cerulean as the alpine lake from which she'd just emerged. A summer co-op student from Stockholm, she was studying to be a geologist, something Burt had once thought he would be.

"Why not hike the Rockies?" Burt had asked her the day before.

"It is this older landscape that interests me, and besides the Alps are but a skip away from Sweden," she'd said with a dainty snort. Her English was competent though her idioms muddled. Burt found it charming, but later Melody, his wife, had hissed in his ear, "European snob."

With his eyes on Tilde, Burt now took a bagel from Melody, who sat beside him on the rocks with the rest of the small group. The cream cheese functioning as an adhesive between the bagel's top and bottom did little to mitigate the dryness. Burt gulped from his water bottle.

Tilde settled on a large scree boulder apart from everyone. Burt imagined the rock beneath her buttocks tossed from some glacier millenniums ago.

"It's not about the destination, it's about the journey," Melody said to Sandy, a middle-aged woman sitting next to her. Hiking trips, perhaps stirred by the negative ions in the mountain air, moved his wife to pop philosophy. She reached into a Ziploc bag full of nuts, fat raisins and tiny chocolate chip nipples, made a joke about expanding hips and menopause. The giggle that once rang through his life clean as a chime, now scraped rudely on his senses.

Burt and Melody had been hiking for the twenty-five years of their marriage, though much of that time in the company of their sons. When the boys, in their teens, preferred other activities, Melody took up gardening, so she could be home in case the boys were around. After their oldest son moved out, Burt, hoping to rekindle his wife's interest, brought home a brochure about a hiking club and Melody liked the idea of broadening their social activities.

Burt was after the views. Not an athletic man, he preferred the end of the line, all the time watching for something to photograph. In the fall he would show the photos to his grade eight geography class and point out the Golden Hinde, its jagged superlative peak. His students were at the age where it took the tallest, the biggest, and the best to impress.

Water droplets clung to his nose. He scratched the three-day stubble on his chin, removed his fogged up glasses and rubbed them on the tail of his shirt. When he replaced them on his face he saw that Tilde stood next to him, her narrow feet and burgundy-coloured toenails a few centimetres from where he sat on the ground.

"I have found something that will interest your students," she said, the vowel sounds dredged from the depths of her voice box.

Melody glanced at Tilde and then at Burt. Tilde looked toward the lake, brushed away a black fly. Trying to ignore the weariness in his body, Burt struggled to a standing position.

As he placed his full weight on his feet, he winced with a pain he'd not known before, deep in the flesh of his knee. It had been like this since he started hiking again, the weaknesses in his body revealing themselves. He supposed aging was a kind of turning inside out, all that inner activity coming to the surface.

He followed Tilde along the lakeshore, inhaling the spicy smell of the sub alpine and fiddling with the camera around his neck. They slid down a pile of till striped with snow, out of sight of the others and to the water's edge. She stepped into the shallows near the shore and gestured for him to follow. He sat down on a rock and removed his boots and socks. He was aware of the stench of his feet as much as he was of the fine hairs on her flesh as she scooped water into her hands and released it to cascade down her bare arms.

"How deep?" he asked, rolling up his pant legs.

"Not so deep," she said bending to stare into the water. "Here it is."

The cold clenched his ankles and the rocks beneath his feet were slippery and uneven. He stumbled and winced again at the pain in his knee.

"Okay?" she asked, a smile playing at the corners of her mouth.

He nodded and peered through the reflection of the shrouded mountains on the lake's surface. At first, he could not make out what she was trying to show him and then beneath the water an impression in the limestone emerged: an elongated oval shape wrapped in a line of discs.

"A fossil," he said, looking up at her.

"Cross-section of a crinoid, I think. Yes?" She crossed her arms.

He bit his lip. Running his fingers and thumb down his chin, he said, "I can't say for certain." At Cedar Hill Middle School, he taught trilobites and Albertosaurus.

"I am correct, I think." She uncrossed her arms, sure of herself now. "If this is, in fact, an example, it is from the Permian period. It is 280 million years old. Can you imagine?"

The water stirred where she moved her foot and burgundy flashed from her toes, for a second obscuring the fossil. So, this is what it came down to—a fleeting imprint at the bottom of a lake high in the mountains, a mere trace of life.

"Some things have staying power, I guess." He sounded stupid.

She smiled politely. "I like its other name better. *Water lilies.*"

He wished he had more to say, that he might impress her, and then he remembered something. "Limestone is called *life* stone because of its layers of organisms that lived millions of years ago."

It was as if she hadn't heard him. "It is more beautiful than its scientific name. Water lilies, because they were attached to the ocean floor and had many long arms coming off this stem that we look at. Arms like feathers reaching upward and searching for nourishment." She spread and stretched her fingers in a squeezing action, and her gaze drifted, and then as if she caught herself, she looked fully at him and said, "An echinoderm."

He nodded. "Spineless." He immediately felt he'd said something too personal. She stretched her hand towards him, bent and touched his knee, her fingers brushing the skin. "It is swollen."

It was the first he'd noticed, how one knee was fleshier than the other. "A ski injury from last winter," he said, startled to realize that he, a man not given to lies, had just told a lie. He had no idea what he'd done to his knee—some harm done unnoticed.

"Can you photograph the fossil for your students?" Tilde asked.

Burt was grateful for the change of subject. "If we are very, very still."

Tilde stepped out of the water and stood behind him. Burt leaned forward and opened the aperture on his camera, took a breath and squeezed the shutter as he exhaled. He knew that in the future when he looked at the photograph, it would not be the captured image of the fossil, but the presence of Tilde and the deep silence of the mountains that he would recall.

They woke to rain and prepared breakfast beneath their tarps.

"It'll clear," said Melody, and handed him a pot with the remainders of the porridge after she'd spooned some for herself into a bowl.

The ground was cold beneath him and the oatmeal sticky. He heard a murmur of voices from the others who were not camped far away. Tilde had joined the younger couple in the group, two software designers from Victoria.

"It could rain all day," he said.

"It's hardly rain, Burt. It's more like a mist. Good morning," shouted Melody and waved to Dave, Sandy's partner, and the group leader who walked up from the lakeshore, balancing a full pot of water. He stopped while he and Melody exchanged thoughts on the weather.

Burt kept his head bent to his cold porridge. His wife's voice shrilled out of the morning's quiet discordant as metal on metal, radio static, jackhammers. He sipped his coffee and inhaled a mouthful of grounds, spit them out, slapped at mosquitos. Melody tossed him the Deet. He squeezed a tiny drop on his finger and rubbed it into his temples. Its chemical stink mixed with his body's stink.

"Cowboy coffee, you gotta love it," said Melody, wiping her mouth and laughing.

"I don't love it," he said and pushed himself to his feet. He rummaged through the toiletry bag for his toothbrush and toothpaste.

"You've got that cranky silent thing going this morning, Hon. You'll feel better once we're on the trail."

He scanned his surroundings beneath the sodden cloud cover. A desolate moonscape, uneven black and gray stone with scrubby struggling vegetation. Where was the beauty in this?

He watched Tilde walk away to the edge of the tents and followed her. When he caught up, she was brushing her teeth.

"Do you think we'll see the mountain today?" he asked.

She paused, and with a mouthful of toothpaste responded with a question. "Is it true that the Golden Hinde is the highest peak on Vancouver Island?" With toothpaste in her mouth, her voice brought to mind the soft swish of rain against the window.

"Yes, 2200 metres," he said, pleased to know something that she didn't. While Melody was indifferent to his knowledge, Tilde reminded him of his ignorance. The night before he almost told Melody that Tilde was a smart girl, though she wasn't a girl in the same way that his sons were boys and Melody didn't like her, so in the end he showed his wife the picture of the fossil and said nothing.

A raindrop plopped on the mound of toothpaste on his brush, wobbled and slithered down his hand. He was damp beneath his Gortex, his skin sticky and his feet wet. He shoved the toothbrush into his mouth and brushed hard. Beside him, Tilde also brushed and together they made a bristly sawing sound while the black flies and mosquitos circled and gnawed at their skin. He swallowed and shook out his toothbrush. She spit, and then her laughter, sharp-edged, startled him. "You swallow your toothpaste?" she said.

On the ground, the spit from her mouth bubbled and shone. He looked up at her and winked. "Well, only when I'm hiking. It's a Canadian thing, eh, don't sully the Earth. Primitive, no?" He grunted and leaned toward her.

She laughed louder, blue eyes beneath the hood of her blue raincoat, assessing him and holding his gaze. "You are a funny man." She turned and walked toward the tents. He imagined the strength in that body beneath all the layers of Gortex and fleece, a flat belly and wee, vulnerable breasts.

"Funny ha-ha or funny strange," he called after her.

She glanced at him while she walked, wrinkled her brow, said nothing.

Dave and Sandy, the two leaders, had met only a few years before in the hiking club. Dave's big grin and frequent laughter rotated a full gray-streaked beard up and down and across his jaw. Sandy carried field guides with her, though she knew by heart the names of the wildflowers and the birds. When they set up and broke camp, each action complemented the other: Dave collapsed the aluminum poles while Sandy nested the cooking pots, Sandy turned to help fold the tent, the wordless movement from task to task and like a sleight-of-hand, the tiny sprawl of their campsite amalgamating into two neat backpacks.

When the group was assembled at the trailhead, Dave described the route up to Marble Peak. There were mumblings about the weather, nervous laughter at the suggestion of a cold beer and a warm pub at the base of the mountain. Sandy promised stunning views as soon as the clouds cleared. Dave opened the map, pointing to where they were headed. Melody melted into the group, warm with enquiries about how people slept, quick to laugh at the jokes.

Burt offered to sweep which allowed him to lag at the end of the line, to favour his good leg. He'd slid a neoprene brace over his knee that morning without mentioning it to his wife, coveting the knowledge that Tilde was the only one who knew about the swelling on his knee, and he imagined her asking about it. Falling asleep in the tent the night before, he'd allowed his mind to feel again the feather brush of her fingertips on his skin. With any luck, she would walk with him and he could show her what he knew about the geology. He wouldn't mention that he had read the brochures only the night before. He would tell her that they were walking on a fragile landscape, this karst landscape with its underground erosion. But Tilde darted to the front of the line. Now and then she'd disappear behind a pile of rock and reappear, poised with her camera above or beside a rock face.

The group moved upward while his wife's voice dominated the chatter. It was their way, socially; Melody interpreted their lives, Burt sometimes finished her sentences, clarified and rarely contradicted. The women vied for airtime and Melody was generous enough to accommodate. People opened to Melody. Sometimes he was jealous that she had access in a way that he didn't, to the tender hearts of their sons.

By late morning the rain stopped and the clouds lifted, revealing the lower halves of the mountains. The group drew inward and became silent, the upward trek distilled to footfall, the body, and its weariness. Rock, tree, sky. It was a strange alchemy Burt had seen in their past hiking days; on occasion both he and his wife moved finally to tears for no particular reason. Melody had said it was for the abundance of beauty in their surroundings while he saw it as a sorrow for the scarceness in themselves.

The group took a break at a jagged rock outcropping

and Burt was glad for an opportunity to rest his knee. The clouds collided above them. "We'll get our view yet," said Dave.

Burt stood at the edge of a long drop searching in the sky for patches of blue. Someone stepped up beside him and for a second he thought—hoped—it was Tilde. It was his wife. She laid her hand on his shoulder.

"How are you doing, Hon?"

"Good."

"I thought you might have been limping."

"No. You, how are you doing?"

"I'm talking too much as usual, but you know, I do that, don't I? I'm wobbly, I don't know why, but it's good, it's good to be out here again. The air is so, so startling, isn't it."

He smiled and cast his gaze over the cliff beneath them. "It's a difficult terrain."

"You seem tense, Hon. You used to love this. Are you okay?"

He resisted a brief urge to tell her all about his knee, about being pestered by thoughts of a girl not much older than his sons. He'd never been unfaithful to his wife.

"You always think I'm tense. Relax, enjoy yourself. I'm fine." He kissed her cheek and she reached for a strand of hair spilling from under his cap, wrapped a curl around her finger.

"You're the handsomest man here, Burty," she said in a child's voice, the way she did when she imitated the first graders she taught. She spun like a younger, lighter woman on her heel, and he whispered loudly, "Later."

She turned and wrinkled her nose. "Not in the tent."

Soon the clouds parted enough to give them fleeting glimpses of the mountain. The going was slow. The trail was frequently cut off by deep fissures in the rock, necessitating frequent consultations and a constant search for trail markings.

At the rest stop, Burt watched Tilde add a stone to a cairn.

"Do you have Inukshuks in Sweden?"

She startled and two stones fell at her feet. "Look what you've done." She replaced the stones. "Do you mean stone men?"

He shrugged and nodded.

"Of course. I believe the word is inunnguaq, a cairn representing a human figure."

"You must be good at Trivial Pursuit." He regretted saying it. He didn't mean for it to sound insulting. He didn't know what he meant.

"Do you think knowledge is trivial, Burt?" she asked tilting her head.

"No, yes. Sometimes it's irrelevant and people show off, don't they?"

"Is that what you think I do?"

"I didn't say that. I think you are an intelligent young woman and there is no need to hide your intelligence under a bushel."

"A what?" She laughed.

"Like a bush."

"How is your knee?"

"Oh, my knee." He shrugged. "A little sore, but I just don't think about it. The descent will be the worst."

"It always is."

"And how are your fossils?"

"I've found some brachiopods. Would you like to see?"

He stood next to her and she flipped through the tiny screen of her camera showing him the images of cockle-like shells. There was fineness in her movements, her hair, the shape of her chin and somewhere beneath the confidence, an unmet need.

"My father is a biologist," she said. "I will be a scientist like him."

"Your mother?"

"Dead."

Melody, who always "made an effort," failed to fold Tilde into the cocoon of her affability. "Do you have relatives or friends in Canada?" she asked.

"No."

"Brave girl coming here all on your own. When I was in my fourth year, way back when, I did an exchange for four weeks to London. I was so lonely."

"Excuse me," Tilde had said, heaving her pack onto her back and stepping past Melody.

"Well, aren't we snippety," whispered Melody to Burt.

Though it was unlike her, Melody lost her footing. There was a clatter of tumbling stone, a screech, then Sandy shouted his wife's name. At the bottom of a slope covered in loose stones five or so metres down, Melody lay in a heap curled under her heavy backpack. She was still and silent. Burt pushed down the slope sideways, scattering the small rocks with the edges of his feet.

"I'm coming, Hon," he shouted.

When he got to the bottom, the heap that was Melody uncurled and giggled, a sound as lucid and silver as the air. She had landed in a bank of snow and white crystals clung to her eyelashes. Beneath them, her eyes shone. He removed her backpack and helped her sit up, wrapped his coat around her.

"You're white as a sheet," he said.

Behind them, Dave and Tilde scrambled down. The others stood above on the bank and, reassured that she was okay, fell into conversation. Dave questioned Melody about how she was and behind them Burt stared at Tilde. It didn't seem right, her being here now.

"I have first aid," she said.

"So do I, so does Dave," he said.

"I have wilderness first aid, from Sweden." Her voice was sharp, each word abrupt.

"My shoulder hurts, probably bruised. I'll be okay in a minute," said Melody to Dave, waving her hand.

"No rush," said Dave. "Take it easy."

Tilde, crouched beside Melody and without speaking, eased her t-shirt off her shoulder. She prodded with her finger, bent her arm at the elbow and pulled gently.

"Does this hurt, or this?"

Melody flinched. "There," she said, "and there."

"No swelling yet," said Tilde, but you should not walk. You will faint."

Melody's eyes were dull with pain. Burt handed her his water bottle and urged her to drink.

"I am fine, Tilde. I will be good to go shortly." She sipped the water.

"No, you should not," said Tilde. "Your shoulder is broken."

Melody attempted to get to her feet, wobbled and dropped to her buttocks. "I will decide what I will do." She fixed her eyes on Tilde.

"Tilde has her wilderness first aid," said Burt.

"I don't give a goddamn what she has."

Tilde's lips edged into a half smile. Her eyes flickered from Melody to Burt.

Dave tried his cellphone. "No coverage. Melody, I'm going to get help. I agree with Tilde. You're too weak. I'll send the others on. Sandy knows the route." He turned and hurried up the bank.

"I'm going with them," shouted Melody, attempting to stand again.

Burt placed his hand hard on her good shoulder; she shook it off and glared at him.

"You're not going anywhere but down," he said. He drew her close. She collapsed against him and he eased her to the ground.

"Go Tilde," he said, without looking. "Thanks for your help."

After a minute, the rocks shifted behind them as Tilde climbed back up the bank without a word.

They sat like that for two hours, Melody drifting in and out with her head on Burt's shoulder. He had never known his wife in this wounded, quiet state. The silence was punctuated by the distant screech of a pika, the gusting wind and little else. He had a wide-ranging view of the surrounding landscape. It was hard to believe that what he faced was the result of great geological upheavals, tectonic shifts, an ocean rising and falling, the dissolution of limestone, sinkholes and rivers appearing and disappearing. In the calm of the afternoon it comforted him to know that he and Melody waited amidst the beautiful aftermath of a former time.

Dave led the paramedics up the last two kilometres and they carried Melody on a stretcher to where they had landed the helicopter, all the time Melody protesting that it was too much and unnecessary. When they confirmed that her shoulder was fractured, she grew quiet until Burt said he would collect the tent and their packs, and meet her at the hospital in a few hours. She cried then, finally, and said "Burty, don't leave."

Burt hurried down the mountain, pain like wire wrapping itself around his kneecap. Back at the camp, he stuffed as much as he could into his pack and left the surplus for Dave and the others to carry down. He skirted along the lake, and recalling the crinoid, stopped for only a moment to peer over the water. It was not the fossil but a reflection on the lake's surface that struck him—a remote mountain top, saw-toothed and far above the others. When he turned to look for the real thing, the clouds had shifted.

The Truth about Gravity

Merc lets go of his chainsaw and allows it to bounce on the tether attached to his harness. With both hands free, he fumbles with his fly. Feet against the trunk and arching his back he leans out from a Grand fir, twenty-five metres above Mrs. Gundison's Uplands home. From here, he sees her swimming pool covered in green scum, her Saab and the wide blue ocean. Purple heads of flowers bob in the breeze on the sunny side of the garage. Merc has a hold on his penis now. He takes aim and a golden crescent of urine sparks in mid-air, arcs, and lands with a kind of grace in the plush dahlia bed.

He grunts with satisfaction, shakes, and tucks himself back into his pants. He yanks the pull-cord on the chainsaw and just as he is about to press blade to branch, catches sight of Mrs. Gundison at the side of the garage peering up at him, eyes shaded beneath one hand.

To hell with her and her dead husband's multi-million-dollar chicken industry. He thrusts the screaming saw into the tree. To hell with all women. A gnarled limb jolts skyward then bumps its way to the ground; to hell with Celia, especially, nattering and nattering at him to go work for Troy—*at least he's got his life together*—until she breaks him down. Oh, she breaks him down, all right. Merc's got no prospects so he grovels to Dick-brain and here he is, first day on the job.

Don't screw up, Troy said that morning before going off fishing with his fat brother and a two-four of Lucky. Merc could report Troy to WorkSafe because right now there's nothing but a harness between him and the earth below.

He slices at another branch and the motor drops a few octaves; he shifts and digs his spurs into the tree's swarthy trunk, pushes against the saw with all his weight. The branch tumbles; he lets the motor die and the saw dangles by his side. He leans back, looks down at the miniature world below then tilts his head up to the massive sky. Merc was a climber for ten years before the woods shut down, the best in his crew. On the ground amongst people and things he feels overshadowed and claustrophobic, but from the pinnacle of a conifer facing into the void above, he's weightless. If he had a religion, here would be his temple.

Celia tells him he should come down to earth and grow up. She doesn't like that he lives in the basement of the house where he grew up, even if he gives his mom money when he can. He can't live with Celia because welfare would cut her off if they found out. He wouldn't anyway. There're her brats and he can't stand her neighbours. Celia just ignores them except for Nancy. He doesn't get it—Nancy with her blood-red lips and that *lemme-dig-my-spurs-into-your-Achilles'-heel-Honey* smirk of hers. He tells Celia to get out of there, but she can't afford unsubsidized rent.

By the time he's done, Merc's t-shirt is clammy, his eyes sting and his lips are salty. When he rappels downward, he spots Mrs. Gundinson standing below.

She's shrugging her shoulders and grinning like an excited kid. That's better than watching a tight-rope performance, she says.

His feet touch the ground and he unstraps his gear without looking at her. Glad to entertain you, he says and swipes his forehead with the back of his hand, swigs from his water bottle, points to the hip-deep pile of branches scattered around the tree. I'll take those away with me. She nods, and then they stand for a moment with necks craned up toward where the tree's amputated limbs once reached out, where the light now falls through.

How about an iced coffee? Grinning again, like maybe she thinks it's hilarious he pissed on her dahlias.

Since he's a guy who can't say no to women, he agrees to coffee, though he's pretty sure it means listening to a lecture from the old lady regarding his highwire whizz.

A veil of grey hair shifts around Mrs. Gundison's shoulders and she moves like the branches of a willow as if her limbs couldn't quite fix themselves in space. She's about his mother's age, though his mom plods where Mrs. Gundison floats—his mom with her defeated double chin and dark roots, her penchant for Rocky Road ice cream, how she makes Merc go to the store and pick it up for her.

He follows Mrs. Gundison to a stone patio at the edge of a line of cedars above the shore. Ceramic pots stuffed and overflowing with herbs and flowers, some dried out and dead, are scattered amongst wooden lawn chairs. In its better days, the garden would have been like ones in the magazines Celia borrows from the Neighbourhood House. Celia stuffs plastic pots with vegetables and flowers, puts them on her cluttered patio beside the kids' bikes, broken dump trucks, eyeless dolls. It's beyond Merc how anything can grow when, next door, hookers howl and dealers rant, when some shrill-voiced bitch screams at her social worker. Grow they do, green and healthy amongst the detritus; Celia's got a knack. He loves it when she pops a radish in the mouth of her youngest and he makes that face, how he smacks his mom but then there's all the giggling and hugging and even Merc laughs. When Celia smiles, her overbite is beautiful and the gold flecks in her eyes light up like tiny jewels.

Mrs. Gundison tells him to sit down and he tries to relax in one of the chairs but his muscles are tight and he stinks with sweat. He starts to think maybe he should get his pay and get the hell out of here when he sees a stone Buddha staring at him from between a couple of ferns. The Buddha's eyelids are heavy, but Merc can feel its gaze. Its lips are turned up in an expression of pure serenity and Merc finds himself falling back into the chair as if the Buddha had laid holy hands on his shoulders. He sits up as Mrs. Gundison appears carrying a silver coffee decanter, a bowl of ice, mugs and a plate of Oreos on a tray.

She settles into a chair and pours the coffee. It must be hard work climbing trees like that. She passes him the Oreos.

Yeah. He shoves a cookie into his mouth. She watches him. So, too, does the Buddha. She wouldn't even notice if it was gone. She's likely got more, the yard riddled with them, holy deities hiding in the bushes.

Nice place you got, he says.

It's a lot, the upkeep, you know. Her eyes sweep the waterfront with a rapturous gaze that disintegrates into a frown. My son might come live with me. It's as if she's forgotten Merc's there, and then she swings her head in his direction. Do you get much work?

So long as there's trees.

She laughs. The Buddha watches from the bushes.

Merc's a sucker for laughter. My girlfriend would like your flowers.

Really.

Her voice is surprised, surprised at what, that he has a girlfriend, that any girlfriend of his would have Mrs. Gundison's refined tastes?

What's her favourite flower?

Merc shrugs.

My husband wouldn't have known my favourite flower, either.

Sad, the old lady looks sad. Maybe the guy was a jerk. He clears his throat. I ought to get going.

Oh sure, I'll get your pay. Cash, right?

Whatever Troy said.

As soon as she is out of sight, Merc goes over to the edge of the patio and lifts the Buddha in his arms. The statue is cool against his overheated skin. He walks quickly toward the truck, opens the passenger side door and shoves it onto the floor.

A few minutes later Mrs. Gundison finds him tossing armfuls of branches into the back of the truck. She is carrying a bouquet of purple-headed flowers.

These are for your girlfriend. Dahlias. Her expression is serious, like this is important. She hands over the flowers and a cheque. The cash is for you, she says.

He shoves the roll of twenties into his pocket and takes the dahlias without looking at her, mumbles thank you.

She watches him climb in the truck and waves as he backs out the driveway.

Beside him on the seat, the dahlias are bright and honest. On the floor, the Buddha's smile turns mocking like it's in on some joke at Merc's expense. And then its face becomes Celia's face when she's telling him what to do and what not to do. It's like the Buddha is giving him shit, only it's not the Buddha. It's Celia.

Barely down the block, Merc stops the truck, opens the door, and kicks the Buddha onto the boulevard. Kicks it hard. It goes flying, does a nosedive into the ditch, and Merc spits in its direction, jerks forward then shoves his foot on the brake. He sighs and backs up, jumps out, uprights the Buddha and faces it toward Mrs. Gundison's. As he drives away, he decides he'll buy Celia a garden ornament and the thought of her smile makes him feel airy and light, as if he's falling, falling into the empty sun-charged air.

Filter Feeders

Reaching for her, the ocean loses steam near Bess's feet where it spits rivulets of cold water. With the sound of a hundred deaths crunching under boots she crosses a barnacled beach. There was a time during her undergraduate years that she would have picked her way around them, preventing their death, and recited their name: *Balanus nubilis.*

The bay is sheltered, no surf here. Mounds of damp snow blot the shoreline and up on the bank white lines trace fleshy branches of arbutus. The boy is on the beach again. Flat on his belly beneath the oversized yellow rain-coat he's like a jellyfish smeared on the rocks, something washed from the sea. His hands stroke the surface of a tidal pool. He's not facing her but he knows she's there. He's staring at the barnacles again. They say he's not right, but that's okay—they say she's odd, the way she's alone all the time.

"So what's with the snow, Andy?" she says

"Won't stay," he says. He's about fifteen. He never looks at her. His eyelids are always half-closed.

"I once lived in a place where the ocean froze solid every winter." It doesn't matter to her whether he's interested or not. This is why she likes talking to him.

Andy scans the sea. Patches of snow drift on its surface. "Looks like clouds on the water. Makes it quiet." He shakes his head. "Won't last." His fingers, busy beneath the water, are red from the cold.

She crouches beside him, watches a barnacle open, reach with its feather-like cirri, and then close.

"Watching for the cirri, Andy?"

"Sessile phytoplankton feeders. Filter food through cirri." His hands swirl faster to create a whirlpool.

"What's the life span of the Thatched barnacle?" She taught him that last Saturday. She likes to test him, to see if he remembers.

"Fifteen years." As if suddenly jerked upward by a set of strings Andy rises and walks up the bank toward his house.

In the late afternoon Bess sits on her glassed-in front porch and sips on a Guinness, a habit from the days when her father was alive. In the swirling wind the water on the bay is chaotic with whitecaps. On winter afternoons the south-easterly always comes up the sound, churning and howling like a child having a tantrum, then exhausts itself by early evening. She thinks about Andy three doors down in the crowded mobile home with his mother and two sisters.

Bess only comes on weekends. Five more years at the marine station and she can retire with a full government pension. Then who knows? She likes sitting here staring out at the water the way her father did but what she doesn't like about Barclay Bay is the way people butt into your business. People like Jen, Andy's mom.

Ever since Jen found Bess' dad dead of a heart attack in the garden she thinks this makes her and Bess friends. It's not that Bess isn't grateful that Jen was here, that someone was here or that she hadn't worried about her father being isolated in Barclay Bay, though he never seemed to need anything except Bess's company on weekends. It's just that now when Bess pushes her grocery cart through Jen's till at the Co-op she hears all about Andy: the special aide he has at school, the tantrums, the fire setting. Once Jen told her the psychologist said that people like Andy have difficulty filtering out sensation. Surely, there couldn't be other people like Andy.

The way she's always smiling even when she talks about the horrible things the boy does you'd think that Jen's in control of the situation. The poor woman has to be a martyr. Why doesn't she put the boy in a home?

Jen makes mobiles out of shells she gets her children to collect from the beach. Bess has seen rotting piles of bivalves on the bank in front of Andy's place. She tells the boy to take only the abandoned shells. After Bess' dad died Jen gave her one of these mobiles. There was something too intimate about the gift and it wasn't just that Bess got few gifts. It was that Jen clearly didn't understand about bivalves, how the insides of these shells supported life in the same way that the human skeleton does, only in reverse. Hanging the mobile would have been like hanging a skeleton of her father in the living room.

Bess drifts off and wakes to a rapping at the screen door. She hears the door open and Jen calling her from the kitchen. Bess stumbles toward the light switch and the dim overhead floods the tiny living room. "In here," she shouts, rubbing her eyes.

When Jen steps into the light her tear-streaked face is covered with mascara. Groggily, through Jen's blubbering, Bess gathers that Andy is missing.

"Enough. Tell me what happened," says Bess, echoes of her father in her own voice. He wouldn't have tolerated sniveling of any kind, not that Bess had ever been inclined toward tears.

"It was a bad tantrum, but it wasn't because of having

to go away. The psychologist said that children like Andy don't feel things the same way we do, don't attach themselves emotionally."

Bess can't help but think of barnacles, how they anchor themselves to rocks, Andy saying the word, *sessile*, that afternoon in his monotone voice.

"I've arranged for him to live in a group home in Victoria. They have better services there. You have no idea what it's like and I have to think of the girls. If we could just go to a lousy movie once in awhile. I never get a break." She wails again.

Over a movie, thinks Bess who never goes to movies, but she knows it's not just that. When women cry around her, as if she lacks some important female hormone, she feels inferior.

What the hell is that strange child up to now, and why does Jen have to involve her? She runs her hands through her hair and remembers something. "He followed me to the headland the other day," she says. She glances at her watch. "The tide is just now starting to go out. How long has he been gone?"

"About three hours."

Bess hates how desperate the woman looks with her smeared make-up and runny nose, how she hangs on Bess' every word. She can't look at Jen. Instead she stares into the black window where she sees only the oblique reflection of the room.

"If he stayed until high tide there'd be no way out. He'd have enough land that he would be safe but sheer cliff behind him," says Bess.

Jen's eyes are wide and watery. Her top lip quivers as if she's about to cry again.

"My kayak is on the beach. I could be there in fifteen minutes." Bess hasn't eaten and now her dinner will be late. Not that it's much; a can of sardines, some rye crackers, what her father and she used to eat Saturday nights. It's cold in the house, with the fire not yet lit, and it'll be even colder on the water. What could that crazy kid be thinking? It would be like him to run out without a coat or shoes but she won't ask the mother because that'll set her off again.

On the beach Jen clutches Bess' blanket around her shoulders. Bess hollers again that she should wait at home but Jen remains fixed, still as a heron, and uncharacteristically silent. Bess sighs and guides the kayak out into the bay. She has to come back with the kid—they are now at one another's mercy, she and Jen.

The wind dies as Bess knew it would, and a half moon appears and then disappears behind the last of the clouds. The snowstorm of the night before has passed but the weather could go either way now. It's always like that on the water, the clouds and the wind nervous and indecisive. Bess is chilled, in spite of the wet suit she wears under her father's bulky sweater and the wool toque knitted for her by a Kwakiutl elder who felt sorry for her because she'd never had a mother. Bess had stayed with her while working on a research project, and she had been regaled with stories of the old woman's six children and fifteen grandchildren. As Bess paddles she thinks about mothers; about Jen and how foolishly motherhood makes her behave, and about herself, what kind of a mother she might have been. Sometimes she imagines herself as a mother but not very often anymore. She couldn't love a child the way that Jen does; stupidly, noisily, messily, the way they seem to need to be loved.

Andy was right about the snow not staying. It never does. This, after all, is the temperate rainforest where it never gets too cold or too hot, a sodden world of indiscriminate greens and browns, grey skies. Clouds scuttle across the moon turning the shoreline to a black shifting shape where isolated flickering lights illuminate nothing. On the largeness of the ocean's surface the lamp fixed to the kayak's bow casts a sombre glow and the only sound is the splash of the paddle. The cold air stings Bess' cheek. It's possible she won't recognize the headland in the dark. It's possible the boy won't be there which means she's entirely alone out here. She once had a co-worker who got turned around in the dark on the sea, lost his sense of direction and went too far offshore when a wind came up... but it must have been a moonless night, and no one knew for sure what happened. They'd found his bloated body and overturned kayak the next day. How alone he must have felt.

The headland had to be near now but nothing is familiar. Beaches are dangerous at night where it would be easy to trip on a log, fall and bang your head. Knocked out you wouldn't know the tide was coming in or if you had a broken leg? Stupid kid. If he was there on that headland what was she going to say to him? She didn't want to spook him and make him run off in the dark. He was lucky and he didn't even know it. Lucky to have a mother. She could tell him that but she doubted it would make any difference. And how did she know he was lucky to have a mother? To her mothers had always seemed like fussing, overbearing creatures. Her father had never been like that. She supposed he'd loved her though he'd never told her so. When she was a child he made dinner for her every night, took her to the library on Saturdays and on Sunday afternoons sat with her for hours staring into tidal pools, saying nothing. When she finished her postgraduate degree he came to her convocation and took her for dinner afterwards. He gave her an expensive Gortex jacket and pants to match. "To keep you dry in the rain," he said. She'd taken that for love.

Now in sight, the peak of the headland has a distinctive hooked shape, more obvious in the dark. She drags the paddle deep in the water and rounds the steep bank. Just as she'd estimated, the tide is high, the water snugged up against the cliff and the beach submerged. The moon comes into view and a smattering of stars tremble between the clouds. In a tiny bay on the other side of the headland she makes out a figure in yellow hunched on the shore.

With a bang Bess pulls the kayak up onto the rock shelf but Andy doesn't stir from where he crouches before a tidal pool. She wonders what he can possibly see in the dark.

"An arthropod's got an exoskeleton," he shouts.

"What's it for?" she asks, walking towards him.

He shrugs.

She crouches beside him and resists the temptation to brush his hair from his eyes. "To protect its soft insides," she says. They stare for what seems like hours at clusters of barnacles gleaming in the moonlight. The tide is receding.

Then he stands up, stumbles toward the waterline and lifts an oyster off the beach, holding it above his head. "The bivalve mollusc stays hinged with a large adductor muscle." His voice is monotone. "Sometimes grows pearls, carries barnacles on its back and a pearl inside." She wonders if this is for her benefit, to show her what she has taught him.

"Not all of them have pearls, Andy."

"Don't know unless you look." He counts the barnacles on the oyster's shell, and then drops it into the pool. "Nobody looks," he says.

Finally she says, "Would you like to come spend some Saturday nights at my house?"

At first he's silent and she thinks he doesn't understand and that it's probably for the best, but then he brushes his hand through the chilly water and says, "To look at crustaceans?"

Andy helps Bess place the kayak high up on the shore behind some logs for safekeeping until she returns at daylight.

The tide has pulled far enough away from the land to free the passage home along the beach. On the way back Andy swings his long legs forward and chants, "to look at crustaceans on Saturday nights."

Fenced In

Chap, named for El Chapo, the uncatchable Mexican drug lord, jerked his compact body along the chain-linked fence and jabbed his nose into the space where a bar of metal met the hard dirt. Behind him in the large yard twenty or so dogs mingled, snouts to ground, to genital, tails wagging. A sharp bark met a blunt retort and so it went back and forth. Some sprawled, silent and heavy-eyed, on the edge of the mass, watching and sniffing at the moist October air.

Bel and Amy stood outside the fence. "He wants to escape," said Bel.

"He's a street dog from Tijuana, never been fenced in." Amy was big boned and the way she stood with her arms crossed and her feet apart, she brought to mind a tree trunk. After high school, around the time Bel got pregnant, Amy had left the valley. While Bel was raising a son on her own and working at the Credit Union, Amy taught English in Thailand, trekked in Nepal, and volunteered at a school in Mexico. All those years, she sent photos, not of the sights, but of half-starved dogs who roamed the streets. A few years ago, she came back and bought the shelter.

"He needs a home," she said.

The dog was a runt, his feet too big for his body. Surely he'd run. "Why me?"

"To get your mind off those shits you live with." Amy

put two fingers in her mouth and whistled. "Chap, get over here. Come."

Amy was right about Marco, Bel's boyfriend, well, right in ways, but not totally. On the other hand, as mad as Bel got at him sometimes, Jordy had been the constant in her life for sixteen years and he rocked her world, lately in a shredded, painful way, but, regardless, a mother has a responsibility to defend her kid. "Cool it, Amy. You're talking about my son."

Amy leaned on the fence and faced Bel. "You know I love The Jord, but he's become a malcontent, making your life miserable and his even worse. I liked him better when he was a nerd, loved him when he was a nerd, actually, sweet fucking kid." She pushed a fist into her hip and shouted. "Come here, Chap Baby," smacked her thighs and the dog barreled across the yard toward her. She opened the gate and slipped into the yard, Bel behind her. Chap leapt at Amy and she rolled him on his back and rubbed his belly with her big hand. The dog sighed.

"Hey Chap." Bel clicked her tongue to get the dog's attention, but he arched his head to look behind him and above him, anywhere but at her. "Amy, go easy on Jord. He's a teenager. It'll pass."

"Not till Hulk Marco passes, passes like a kidney stone." Amy laughed at her own joke.

Across the yard the hackles of a stout wide-jawed dog went up and a low growl came from deep in its body. Directly in his path another dog with ribs that rippled under its skin rose its narrow snout to the sky and sniffed. Amy stood. "Hey!" Amidst a cacophony of growls, and a blur of muscle, teeth and claw, a tumbleweed of dog spun toward them. Amy strode across the yard, grabbed the bigger one's collar and shoved him into a smaller attached compound.

"Are you taking Chap or not?" She shouted in Bel's direction.

On the way home in the car, Chap paced in the back seat. As she headed south on the inland highway toward home she did what she'd been doing lately when she was alone in the car, and that was pretend she was driving away from Jordy and Marco, Amy and the Comox Valley. In her mind, she heard her car bumping onto the ferry leaving the island for good. A couple months ago she'd looked up a map of BC on Google and traced a route deep into the interior that wound its way through the mountains then north. She'd always wanted to go north, imagined it an uncomplicated place. After a while, she'd go south again, to the prairies where she'd heard you can see a long way; she'd keep going. It would never happen; it's just that she was tired of Marco, somedays of Jordy, and mostly of herself as a mother.

Chap scrambled over the armrest toward her. She blocked him with her forearm and yelled at him. He backed up and curled into a corner of the seat. She told herself it was because of Jordy she took the dog, that maybe it would please him, maybe it would make things better between them. Hadn't everything she'd brought home since he was born been for Jordy: Bunny pasta, every kind of vegetable she'd had to cram into him—she was a good mother—and now and then chocolate-covered donuts from Tim's, running shoes and bicycles, Disney DVDs. Last year it had been an electric guitar. Everything she'd brought through the front door of their double wide for the past sixteen years: hadn't it all been for Jordy? From the back seat came a low grievous howl.

Juggling two bags of groceries and the dog, Bel fumbled her way up the two steps to the front door. Chap wrapped his leash around her ankles then performed a balletic twist in midair toward the grocery bags. Bel landed on her ass on the cement. The dog rolled on his back, spun to sitting position, shook his head and still wouldn't look at her.

"Asshole." Bel got to her feet and gathered up spilled groceries. She yanked at Chap's leash until he yelped and followed her into the house. Inside the door, they met Jordy; he stood in beaten up Blundstones slipping on a plaid jacket. He was so tall now, he had to drop his head to make eye contact with her—usually he didn't bother. Chap leapt at his long legs. Jordy straightened his glasses. Tufts of hair sprouted from patches of pimples on his chin.

"Down, Chap." She undid the dog's leash and he dropped to the floor, stuck his nose into a pile of shoes.

"Chap?" He grinned. "Yours?"

"Well, Amy, you know. He doesn't bark. Weird, hey."

"What were you thinking?" Jordy leaned down to scratch him behind the ears.

"I wasn't," said Bel. "You don't think about these sorts of things."

Beneath his glasses, Jordy raised his eyebrows just as Chap lifted his leg and pissed on his foot.

The first time Bel took Chap for a walk, the dog walked on his hind legs with his head held high and his nose twitching. When she tugged on the leash enough to get him back on all fours, he shoved his nose into the ground and jerked one way then the other like a remote-control car. She imagined him sniffing out rats in Tijuana, ravenous, blood spurting from his mouth as he tore into their flesh.

"Don't let there be any tension on the leash," shouted Amy at the first dog training class. "Walk. Stop, turn as soon as there is tension."

There were six other dogs, fluffy eager-to-please puppies, patient owners who let their dogs sleep on their beds, called themselves Mommy and Daddy.

Jordy helped her patch up the fence with chicken wire, grumbling the whole time. "I don't know why you got such a stupid dog, Mom."

"You can't tell what they're going to be like until you get them home. He'll be ok. He just needs time."

"That's what you said about Marco, but fair enough, the dog is smarter than him."

"Come on, Jord. We've been through this. He tries. He brought you home weights."

Jordy dropped back on his heels. "What am I supposed to do with weights?"

"I don't know. Lift them. I don't know any more than you what people do with weights. Ask him. He's trying."

"He said there's no such thing as climate change."

"That's what you're fighting about these days?"

"Do you have any idea what the emissions are on his fucking Ford Raptor?"

"You googled it, looked it up, right?" She couldn't help but smile at his cleverness, his social conscience—where'd he get that from? "He loves that stupid truck. Why does it matter?" She kneeled on the lawn and unrolled a section of chicken wire. "Have you got the hammer?"

"I looked it up, Mom, I did. What's wrong with that?" He dropped the hammer near her and strode toward the house.

"Emissions are hardly a deal breaker, Jord." She was shouting after him again.

"Not for you, maybe." He pushed the front door open and Chap darted between his legs, headed for the open gate.

What Bel liked about the training is that it required absolute concentration, so that soon she forgot about the other dogs, the smell of beef liver on her hands, what she might go home to after class. Every moment was reduced to a transaction between herself and Chap, as balanced and pure as an equation; hand gesture plus command equals response plus reward.

"Repeat," called Amy, as she roamed between the dogs, and Bel felt an energy flow from her hand through the leash to Chap, as if they were attached. One day he looked at her full on, his head tilted upwards, expectant.

"Sit," she said and he did. "Down," she said, and he lay down. She placed the beef liver on the grass in front of him. "Leave it," she said and he did.

That afternoon on the way home from training class the rain started. Bel pulled into the driveway and parked behind the Ford Raptor. She hustled Chap out of the backseat, patted his head and told him he'd been a good boy. He disappeared into the shrubbery along the driveway. A din, part electronic drone of the kind Jordy plugged into his ears, part human voice, high-pitched, pressed at the door from the inside out, and for a moment she imagined the door bursting outward followed by a pinwheel of arms and legs encircled by punctuation marks in place of human language. Her life had become a cartoon.

Inside Marco and Jordy lay in a heap on the living room floor, limbs tangled around each other so at first she wasn't sure whose thigh and whose bicep belonged to whose body; her boyfriend's or her son's. Jordy's cursing rattled above Marco's incantations: "Trust me, I'm not going to hurt you, Bud." It could have been a hug.

"Hey," the word blasted out of her mouth just as Bel realized it was a command she'd learned that day in dog training. Marco rolled away from Jordy and laughed.

"Just horsing around," he said.

"Hell we are," said Jordy. He staggered to his feet, grabbed his glasses, and planted a swift kick in Marco's ribs.

Marco grunted and gripped Jordy's forearm forcing him to the floor.

"Leave him alone," said Bel. She lunged toward Marco, tugged at the collar of his shirt.

"Fucking ape," said Jordy, spraying spit on Marco's face and just missing his mother.

Marco let him go and got up. He swiped his hand across his mouth, caught his breath. "I was showing him a half-nelson," he said. "Just having some fun." His double chin wobbled. "He thought it was funny until I had him pinned."

"What is the matter with you?" Bel's voice came out hoarse as if she'd been screaming for a long time.

Marco tilted his head making him look like a pug in the training class. He sighed, walked around Jordy and Bel to the fridge, swung it open and grabbed a beer. "Can't do anything right around here."

"Low life," said Jordy, extending his middle finger. His chest heaved up and down, voice pinched as if he were close to tears.

Bel reached for him. "Jord, you okay?"

"Fuck off, Mom." He swung away from her, shoved on his boots and pushed open the front door.

"I'm sorry." She followed him. "Okay, I'm sorry," she screamed at his back. She slammed the door. She was shaking.

Marco sucked on his beer, burped. "I try, Hon, you know I try. I thought it would be fun. You know, man to man, wrestle it out." He punched the air. "In fun, just horsing around. Jord's got no sense of humor. He's serious like you."

She collapsed into a chair at the kitchen table, pulled her knees to her chest, pressed her face to the window. In the waning rain-drenched light Chap bolted from behind a bush and ran towards Jordy wagging his tail. Her son leaned down and scratched under the dog's chin, said something to Chap and slipped out the gate. Chap sat with his back to Bel, his head turned in the direction where Jordy walked away. Jordy would be seventeen this year.

"About the dog, Marco."

"The dog?" He dropped into a chair opposite her.

"I've been thinking. It's cruel what we're doing to him: fencing him in, forcing him to obey, be someone he's not. He's used to going where he wants when he wants, living by his wits, giving it all, keeping his head down when he has to. You know, survival: he had it down to an art. We've robbed him of that edge for this? You can't do that to a living thing."

Marco dropped his head low on his shoulders and wrinkled his brow. His double chin wobbled. "He's a dog. Jesus, Babe. We got bigger problems here, and by the way, you got nothing to be sorry about."

"I'm taking Chap for a walk."

"I should just clear out. Right. That's what you're saying. Just say it." His voice like a whimper followed her out the door.

She cornered Chap at the garage and tossed him in the backseat of the car. He fell off the seat and yelped. She had thought of Marco as straightforward, predictable, like one of Pavlov's dogs, unlike her and her son. She thought maybe he'd be good for Jord, a guy's guy, straight up; isn't that what boys needed? She liked that Marco adored every banal thing that came out of her mouth, that he told her she was smarter than him, that he was in awe of her son, at least at first. When she met him, it had been years since she'd slept with anyone, and for a big man, he was gentle.

Chap barked once then was quiet. She watched him in the mirror watching her.

She pulled onto the inland highway and accelerated to 130. There was no traffic. She was angry; at who? The rain swirled across the highway, and a deep puddle grabbed the tires. For a second it felt like the car floated above the road. When her tires gripped the pavement again, she slowed down.

She drove south toward a popular dog walking place she knew. She liked to take Chap there because she could put him on a long line and he could run up the rutted logging road without having to be on a leash. If he got too far ahead or veered too much in the wrong direction, she'd stomp on the line, reel him in as if he were a fish on a hook. It took a lot of nagging and correcting, so it wasn't much of a walk for her, but she told herself the more they practiced the more likely he'd get used to it. And one day he'd run free beside her, maybe.

A few years ago, Jordy and she had gone mountain biking here, but then when Jordy got older he complained about the clear cuts and the logging company that leased the land. He wanted to stay home and play his guitar and watch the next episode of *Game of Thrones*. He was different from her that way. She liked the half-torn forest, the scruffy Scottish broom that overtook the mounds of rotted trees and underbrush. Sometimes there were the remains of a deer carcass left by a hunter for the birds and cougars to pick clean. She parked in front of the yellow iron gate from which hung a *No Trespassing* sign. She and Chap ducked around the gate and set off up the logging road. Rain encircled them: a sodden, swollen shroud. Bel snapped up the hood of her raincoat, glad she'd had the forethought to slip on her rubber boots. There was no one around. Who would be so stupid? It was late in the day and the road was pockmarked with muddy pools through which Chap scampered, tail wagging wildly, nose twitching. She wouldn't go for long, an hour maybe, enough time to work off some steam, figure out what to do. She knew the right thing to do; wasn't that what she'd always done. She felt tethered on all sides. It was hard to think with Chap, all the stopping and correcting.

After about fifteen minutes, they turned up a road that was no longer used except by dog walkers and hikers. It was grassy and uneven, overgrown in places. The Scotch broom hadn't made it this far. She stopped while Chap slurped up water from a puddle. The rain eased.

Thoughts ping ponged in her head as if they came down from the rain-ridden trees. Thoughts like Marco and Jordy not being there at the trailer when she got home as if they'd never been there, how she wished she wouldn't miss them or feel bad about how she'd failed them, mostly Jordy who she knew she owed the world to, something she'd never been able to give him, never would.

When she stopped thinking about Chap or watching him, he got tangled. As the bush thickened around them, it was easy enough to do with the long line snaking through the underbrush and getting wrapped around old stumps. Bel untangled him a few times trying not to lose her temper, but the fourth time she had to release the line from his collar. He bolted.

He burrowed like a rodent through the underbrush. At first Bel followed the rustling sounds he made, stumbling and calling his name, waving a bag of treats, but he got well ahead of her in no time. Further through the trees, she caught glimpses of him leaping above the brush, front and hind legs stretched forward and backward in a gesture of complete trust in the place where he might land. Then he disappeared and finally, she couldn't keep up. She collapsed onto a stump and caught her breath. Her jeans were soaked and so was her hair. She could no longer hear Chap. She hollered for him again, but her voice fell feeble in the silence. All there was to do was wait. And listen.

Clouds collided above revealing patches of blue. Far below the inland highway carved its way through the trees south toward Nanaimo and the ferry. And east of the highway out on the sound Denman and Hornby Islands floated in the blue green ocean.

The silence startled her. Not a rustle of bushes, not the sound of an animal. It was as if the dog had vanished in thin air. He was gone and there was only this silence, this absence of her commands and admonishments. And the most startling thing was that it wasn't like the silence had arrived like a stranger. The silence had always been there; there and likely everywhere, even out on the highway beneath the roar of cars and in faraway cities below the wail of starving dogs, and in the houses under the violent competitions between men and boys, and beneath her own hand where it gripped white-knuckled on the leash.

All these times on the mountain, and she'd missed it; silence as big and deep as the mountain itself. She felt her body relax in spite of her worry about Chap and the chill on her damp skin.

After almost an hour of listening, she hollered for the dog again then thrashed through the bushes in the direction he had gone. In a few minutes, she gave up and made her way back to the main logging road. It was possible he'd returned to the car. Sometimes dogs found their way back to their masters, but she doubted Chap was that kind of dog or that she was a master. The sun was sinking behind the mountain.

He wasn't at the car. There was nothing she could do. She drove toward home, leaving the mountain behind her. Anything could happen to a dog alone out there. He might be attacked by a wild animal, break a leg or starve to death. He might find his way home.

Acknowledgments

Thank-you to their editors of the following journals where earlier versions of these stories appeared:

"The Truth About Gravity." *Malahat Review*, Winter 2013
"Can't Go Wrong with an Iris." *Antigonish Review*
"Exposure." *PRISM International*, Fall, 2013
"Filter Feeders." *grain magazine*, 36.2, 2009

Also, thanks to Oolichan Books: Carolyn Nikodym for keeping me in the loop and her persistence in seeing this book to fruition, and Ron Smith who edited with a discerning and knowledgeable eye along with seemingly necessary doses of reassurance.

I'm grateful to Bill Gaston and Stephen Price for their impeccable understanding of how story works and Lorna Crozier for her deep knowledge and delight in language. All of them taught me well, and so too did Caroline Adderson who one summer helped me transform one hundred raw pages of prose into several of the stories in this book.

I'm also grateful to Arleen Paré, Cornelia Hoogland, Francis Backhouse and Rhona McAdam, whose encouragement, wisdom and advice mean the world to me.

And with loving gratitude I acknowledge my parents, Al and Rose LeBlanc, who first took me on the water and Brian Latta who continues to take me there.

Photo: Karen McKinnon, McKinnon Photography

Judy LeBlanc's short stories have been published in numerous literary journals including *Filling Station, The Malahat Review, Prism, Antigonish Review* and *Grain*. She was recently longlisted for the Prism Short Fiction contest, and in 2015 she won the Islands Fiction contest. In 2012 she won the *Antigonish Review*'s Sheldon Currie Fiction contest, and was longlisted for the CBC Short Story Prize. She has written reviews for *The Coastal Spectator* and the *Malahat Review*.

She teaches English and Creative Writing at North Island College and she is a founding member and artistic director for the Fat Oyster Reading Series.